suspense

HIL   Hill, Reginald.

           The spy's wife

THE SPY'S WIFE

Also by Reginald Hill

A Pinch of Snuff
Ruling Passion

Molly Keatley

BRITISH PASSPORT

UNITED KINGDOM OF GREAT BRITAIN
AND NORTHERN IRELAND

C 0012

THE SPY'S WIFE

REGINALD HILL

 PANTHEON BOOKS, NEW YORK

41,305

Library of Congress Cataloging In Publication Data

Hill, Reginald.
   The spy's wife.

   I. Title.
PZ4.H64856Sp   823'.914   80-7929
ISBN 0-394-51402-5

Manufactured in the United States of America

FIRST AMERICAN EDITION

THE SPY'S WIFE

I

At nine o'clock on an early September day of mist and promise, Molly Keatley was washing the breakfast dishes when she heard the front door open.

'Sam, is that you?' she called.

There was no reply but she heard footsteps move rapidly across the entrance hall and up the creaky stairs. Drying her hands on the tea-towel, she went out of the kitchen and stood in the hallway. Through the open front door she could see her husband's blue Datsun parked so close to the edge of the narrow drive that one of her favourite rose-bushes had been all but uprooted as he got out.

'Oh Sam!' she said with irritation and went out to inspect the damage.

Footsteps clattered down the stairs and Sam Keatley appeared in the doorway.

He was a stocky short-necked man whose normal expression was one of sleepy amiability. His hair was thick and wiry but prematurely grey for a man of forty-four. In times of stress he ran his fingers through it obsessively.

His left hand was harrowing away now and in his right he carried a small suitcase.

'Look what you've done,' Molly said.

'I'm sorry,' he said, tossing the case on to the passenger seat.

'Back the car off, then help me get it back on an even keel. You've ruined all those buds.'

'I'm sorry,' he repeated, climbing into the driving seat.

'I wouldn't mind but there's plenty of trains. Why all the hurry? What had you forgotten anyway?'

'I'm sorry,' he said for the third time.

It began to occur to her that the object of this repetitious apology was not just the rose-bush.

'Sam,' she said.

'I'll get in touch,' he said. 'I love you.'

He slammed the door, trapping a cluster of leaves. As the car reversed violently down the drive, a flowering shoot was ripped off the bush and it was this she always recalled later, not Sam's uncharacteristically pale and set face through the distancing glass. Uncharacteristic too was the ferocity with which he sent the Datsun hurtling down the suburban avenue and round the corner towards the arterial road.

Molly stared in wonder after him, dimly apprehending something momentous. The empty avenue curved away between green-hedged villas, quiet and sinister as an old film set. Then a dog padded purposefully out of a gateway and a milk-float whined along the gutter.

Now only the bright wound on the rose-bush told her Sam had been home.

2

At nine-thirty the door bell rang.

The man on the step was young, late twenties at the most. He was casually but smartly dressed in a suit of faded denim and his blond hair was sculpted in a single wind-swept wave that you could have gone surfing on.

Molly regarded him in silence, knowing that here was trouble certain as a War Office telegram.

'Mrs Keatley?' he said with the accent and intonation of good English breeding. His mouth wouldn't have needed much encouragement to re-arrange itself in a boyishly charming smile.

Molly gave it none, but nodded, blank-faced.

'Is your husband at home, Mrs Keatley?' he enquired courteously.

She shook her head.

'May I step inside for a moment?' he said. 'Just for a moment.'

She opened her mouth, couldn't speak, swallowed, opened it again to beg to be told, please, what was going on. Hysterics wouldn't have surprised her.

Instead she heard herself asking coldly, 'Are you selling something?'

'No,' he said, taken aback. 'Please, just for a moment. Look.'

He was showing her a card. It had his photograph fixed to it, overstamped like a passport picture. On it he looked older, more harassed.

'No, thanks,' she said. 'I've got an album full of old snapshots.'

She did not know why she was saying these things. Her normal doorstep manner was polite, conciliatory almost. Brush salesman and charity collectors went away happy, and there had been times when even Mormons and Witnesses had got enough courtesy to bring them back, reinforced, at night to be turned away by an exasperated Sam.

The blond man, whose name, printed alongside his photograph, was Aspinall, frowned uncertainly as though he too were surprised at the change. Now he looked more like his picture.

'I'm sorry,' he said. 'It would help. It's about your husband. I'm a sort of policeman.'

He held out the card once more. Molly ignored it but turned on her heel and marched through into the lounge. When she turned he was right behind her.

'Thank you,' he said. 'Has Mr Keatley been back this morning?'

She didn't answer. She did not know what an answer might do.

'He left at his usual time to drive to the station, didn't he? What I mean is, has he been back since then?'

She opened her mouth as if to speak but nothing came out so she closed it again. Now he did give her the boyish smile, full of charm, and said, 'Look, Mrs Keatley, it just saves the embarrassment of asking the neighbours.'

She gave an amazed laugh, a single incredulous bark. What kind of pressure did he think he was applying? This was yesterday's threat. This was being sent to bed without any supper.

He took the sound for an encouragement and this time he was right.

'He *has* been back, hasn't he?' he urged.

'Yes,' she said. Not because of the neighbours, but because the laugh had left this new woman ready to take a faltering step towards finding out what had happened.

Aspinall looked more relieved than his certainty should have required.

'May I,' he said, 'may I pop upstairs and may I use your phone?'

He left the room without waiting for an answer and closed the door quietly behind him. It seemed odd that he should want to use the loo so urgently, thought Molly as she listened to his feet ascending the creaky stairs and tried not to think

8

of Sam. Then she heard his footsteps in the bedroom above her and when she opened the lounge door, she could hear other doors opening and closing with swift efficiency and no attempt at stealth.

Aspinall came down the stairs and smiled at her again.

'I won't be a tick,' he said, closing the lounge door in her face.

She heard him pick up the phone receiver and begin to dial. She waited till the dialling had finished and he had begun to speak before she threw open the door and stepped out into the hallway to listen.

He glanced round at her but his flow of words was uninterrupted.

'Yes, he's been back. We were right. At least that cuts down his start. I'm sorry, but Freddie got on the train and it's non-stop to Liverpool Street. He got it stopped at Shenfield. No, not without pulling the cord. I was nearly at Brentwood by the time he got through to the car. Half an hour at least. Yes, I dare say we did pass, thank you very much. No, she hasn't. I'm not sure. Yes, she is. How long? OK, I'll wait till he gets here. See you.'

He put down the receiver.

'I think I would like to ring my solicitor,' said Molly. She watched him closely to assess his reaction.

'I was about to suggest it, Mrs Keatley,' he said. 'It might help.'

He stepped away from the phone and motioned her forward. She was perplexed. The only solicitor she had any knowledge of was the one that Sam had selected, apparently at random, to go through the lease when they rented the house eight years before. She would have to look through the papers to find even his name and, besides, he had seemed so antique, it would not surprise her if he were dead.

'Mr Aspinall,' she said, at last reverting to type, 'please. What's this all about?'

'Ring your solicitor,' he urged gently.

'I want to know what's happened before I ring anybody,' she insisted. 'What am I supposed to say? There's a strange man forced his way into my house and he wants me to ring a solicitor?'

9

Aspinall looked at his watch. He was expecting someone to arrive and getting her to ring a solicitor was probably as good a way as any of keeping her occupied. Whoever was coming must carry enough clout not to be worried by some dandruffy conveyancer. For a second she thought of running out into the street and yelling at the neighbours to fetch the police. But to what end? That little plastic-covered card looked potent enough to sort out a lad in a Panda-car.

She felt sick. She was desperate to know what was happening, desperate to remain ignorant; desperate for help, desperate to be left alone; desperate to see Sam, desperate to know that he was safe even if it meant not seeing him.

Images of crime crowded into her mind. *Murder.* Whose? *Embezzlement.* What was there that a journalist could embezzle? *Rape* . . . no, not that, nothing like that – but was a sexual aberration less likely than the others? Sam was in his forties. Not an easy time. Their sex life had not been so good lately. She had made a conscious effort not to press him too hard, but at thirty-three she had begun to feel the years slipping away and wanted to have a child, and soon. He too, he claimed, and yet in the past month or so he had seemed to turn away from her more and more frequently. So she had been wise and not pursued, not nagged, but she had lain awake sometimes and wondered. Now fresh fears rose. Infidelity? Hardly a crime. But some kind of breakdown – young girls. Young boys. Please God, not that!

'Are you all right, Mrs Keatley?' said Aspinall anxiously. 'Please, come and sit down.'

She let herself be led into the lounge and placed on the sofa.

'Shall I get you a drink? Or a cup of tea?' said Aspinall. 'That would be nice.'

He went out and she leaned back and closed her eyes. Aspinall had said he was a *kind of* policeman. Perhaps that was just a euphemism for private detective. Perhaps it *was* simply infidelity (the relief!) and Sam had just left her for another woman, and *her* husband had been having him watched. That would explain . . . hardly anything. The suitcase he'd been carrying, she couldn't recall seeing it before. What had he taken? She ought to check.

She rose and went into the hall. She could hear Aspinall in the kitchen, probably looking for the tea-pot. Cupboard doors were opening and shutting with the same swift efficiency as had marked his progress upstairs. He had been searching. Surely no simple divorce detective would have dared be so blatant?

She picked up the phone and began to dial.

Aspinall appeared before she'd started the second digit.

'Who're you ringing?' he asked.

She continued to dial.

'Hello,' she said. 'Give me the news desk.'

He moved swiftly towards her, snatched the phone from her unresisting hand and put it to his ear for a moment.

'What do you think you're doing, Mrs Keatley?' he said, banging the receiver down on the rest, but keeping his hand on it.

'What's happening to me is news,' she said, control beginning to go. 'I don't know *what* it is but I bet it's news. You won't tell me anything so I'm going to ask a newspaper.'

'Believe me,' he said urgently. 'They won't know anything. Honestly.'

'Then they bloody well ought to know!' she screamed. 'And I bloody well ought to know! Now either tell me or give me that fucking phone.'

She didn't swear much herself and she didn't like people who swore casually and without noticing it. She couldn't have explained why. But now she dimly apprehended that for her these words had been like a pacifist's bullets, stored away and never thought on till violence was the only peace move left.

And the violence was more than verbal. She tried to grab the phone. Aspinall kept his grip on it and she had no chance in a straight tug-o'-war. So she seized his golden hair right in the middle of the Malibu wave and pulled with all her strength screaming 'Tell me! Tell me! Tell me!'

Aspinall must have been in agony but with his head bent forward under the pressure of her grip, he tried to fend her off with one hand, saying all the while, 'Please, Mrs Keatley' and even muttering 'Sorry' when his fingers accidentally pushed against her breast.

'Tell me!' she screamed. 'You fucking bastard, *tell me!*'

'Tell you what, missus?' said a new voice.

Standing in the doorway was another man. He was about Sam's age, but much thinner, with receding black hair, generously oiled and slicked back as though to accentuate the incipient baldness. He wore a dark blue suit a little crumpled, a little shiny, with a brown woollen cardigan with two buttons undone under the jacket. His narrow face was made for the stoic sneer. He looked like the clerk of works on a building site who holds in equal contempt those who employ him and those who are employed.

'Tell you what?' he repeated in a broad Black Country accent.

'Tell me where my husband is,' she said, releasing Aspinall who gasped with relief and began to rearrange his hair.

'As for that, missus,' said the newcomer, 'I'm hoping you'll tell me. But don't be upset. I'll tell you *what* he is just so you can stop pretending not to know. Sam Keatley's a spy, missus. And he's a traitor, missus. And he's probably a dozen other nasty things besides. And if you're going to faint, missus, do it in Mr Aspinall's direction. He's had the schooling for it. I'll be in your living-room when you're ready to talk.'

3

Molly Haddington had been twenty-three when she first met Sam Keatley. Three years before that she had been living with her parents in her home town of Doncaster in South Yorkshire, where she worked as a typist for the National Coal Board. She was also engaged to be married.

She had known her fiancé distantly since their arrival at the same secondary school, and more closely since they started going together when she was sixteen. They had a great deal in common. He played football and badminton in the winter, and cricket and tennis in the summer, and she watched. She genuinely admired his prowess, though she felt he might have admitted and admired her superiority on the dance floor instead of belittling it. To tell the truth, once off the sports field, Trevor looked rather gawky and though he was six months older than she was, he seemed somehow to have stuck at that unformed, indeterminate stage most boys reach about seventeen. When her father opined that there 'weren't much flesh on him', her mother retaliated confidently that the Challengers filled out late and indeed sometimes ran to fat.

Mrs Haddington was very much for Trevor, who had got good 'O' levels and was reputed to be doing very well as a sales-trainee with Don-Flo Machine Tools Ltd. He himself spoke confidently of the future.

'We'll probably have to move around a bit when we're married,' he said. 'You won't mind?'

'No,' she said.

'Once we get into the EEC, the sky's the limit,' he said. 'How do you fancy a flat in Brussels?'

'Nice,' she said.

'Those who are ready'll get chosen,' he said with an almost religious conviction. 'I'm thinking of doing an evening class in Spanish.'

'Is Spain in the EEC then?' she asked, some vague recollection of her 'O' level studies stirring.

He smiled patronizingly and went on about his proposed travels, with which Molly in her turn patronized her fellow typists who were either unengaged or promised to lads whose horizons stopped at Rotherham.

But she could not spend all her time feeling superior to her friends or inferior to her fiancé, and as the months passed and the proposed date of the wedding approached, more and more she found herself lying in bed at night, wondering about the future – not in any analytical logical fashion because that was not her way, but as one might immerse oneself in a steaming tub of water and lie there till it grew grey and cold, yet still find lacking the will to get out.

She was twenty now, physically fully mature and though not beautiful in any of the classical styles, she had a lively attractiveness which won the approval of all and the propositions of many. She was vain enough to be pleased and had Trevor merely reacted to her hints of other admirers with straightforward jealousy, she would probably have quickly relented and enjoyed soothing him. Instead he chose to attack those who admired her, categorizing them individually and generally as notorious lechers, driven by such indiscriminate lust that a kilted Scot was not safe from their advances.

Molly regarded him coldly and some cog in her mind, rusted by years of inactivity both at school and after, moved. In two months' time at the end of March (for tax reasons) they were going to get married. The cog moved again, its teeth catching and gripping and turning in its turn.

The following Saturday night, after a chilly afternoon on the touchline, she rejected more abruptly than was usual his attempts to slip his hand between her legs. She had no real objection to the hand and sheer vulgar curiosity had led her on several occasions to return the compliment. But recently Trevor, either because of some vain self-image or just the sheer frustration of late adolescent lust, had become tediously, almost brutally insistent on trying to go the whole way. She always refused, usually disguising as moral the simple psychological grounds that she did not really want him. She recognized vaguely that inside marriage a sense of duty or, outside, a sense of experiment might in the end be sufficient reason for saying yes, but she preferred to hang on a bit longer in the hope that a sense of desire might also contribute a little.

They quarrelled (as they had done often before), she handed back his ring (as she had occasionally done before); but this time she meant it for real (which she had never done before).

The reconciliation pattern was for Trevor to turn up midway through Sunday morning, sheepishly apologize on the doorstep, be coldly admitted into the hallway and finally forgiven with a chaste kiss, gradually warming up to a passionate embrace with much pressure of his gloved hand against her sweatered breasts and his trousered erection against her skirted thigh before he went home to lunch.

This time she refused to let him over the doorstep and when she felt herself being moved by his genuine surprise and distress, she said, 'I'm sorry, Trev, but honestly it's best for both of us. I mean it, really, this time I mean it,' and she closed the door in his face which she saw for a few minutes, a pink formless blur through the frosted glass, before he turned away and disappeared.

Six months earlier she might have believed that was that, but now the cog had moved and the machinery was in motion and she foresaw that within minutes of putting her fingers on the keyboard the following day, the absence of the ring would be noted, explanations required, strategies discussed, intermediaries appointed, arbitration arranged. Trevor would return, stimulated now by pressure of public interest as well as the pangs of despised love. And she had little faith in her as yet scarcely tested powers of resistance.

After lunch she went out to the call-box on the corner and rang her cousin Rose who the previous year had gone down to work in London and shared a flat in Fulham with four other girls. Rose was delighted to hear from her. She was, she claimed, down to two girls and the rent was going up. As for work, the streets of London were paved with office managers desperate for anything that could type with two fingers and knew which side of a stamp to lick.

15

Two more interviews remained. The first with her parents. Her father, Ivor, was a slow taciturn man who was foreman of the brickworks where he'd worked all his life. It would be days before he would offer a reaction to such a violent change as his daughter proposed. Her mother was the power centre of the family, energetic and fiercely independent to a point where her daughter often felt cut out. She listened carefully to the half pleading, half defiant proposals.

'Right,' she said. 'If you mean it, it's best, and if you don't, it's nowt but two hours' ride back on the train. Our Rosie is a sensible lass and you won't come to much harm with her. We'd best see where we put the big brown suitcase.'

The second interview was at her place of work. They were intrigued, inconvenienced, indignant. Molly had much of her mother's stubborn awareness of her rights. If she was so in-dispensable, why hadn't they paid her twice as much? she asked pertly. She had two weeks' holiday due. It was intended for the honeymoon. Well, she was taking it now in lieu of notice.

Twenty-four hours later she was being made to feel frumpish and provincial by Rose and her flat-mates who managed to convey the impression that here in Fulham was the fulcrum of the swinging 'sixties.

Following Rose's advice and example, she signed on at a temps agency and spent the next three years side-stepping any alliances, either personal or professional, that smacked of per-manence. She had plenty of boy-friends but was far from promiscuous, though her carefully preserved virginity was washed away in the tide of cheap champagne with which she celebrated her twenty-first birthday. The only pain the loss caused her was a strange feeling of guilt at the thought of Trevor, but this she was now able to dismiss as completely illogical, just as a year later she was able to dismiss the pang of jealousy she felt at the news from Doncaster that Trevor had got engaged to Jennifer Buxton, a dark, pretty girl who'd been in the next class down.

Paradoxically, the news of the engagement made her think for the first time of going back home to live. Rose had got married and departed for Bristol, and though she liked the other girls well enough, the stresses of communal living made themselves felt more frequently. Not that she felt any desire to live alone in London which she enjoyed but trusted only like the fox. A couple of years of growing familiarity had been quite inadequate to erode twenty years' conditioning to the idea that bricks and mortar should always come to an end within brisk walking distance. Doncaster calls less seductively than many provincial towns to its errant young, but there were times when its hoarse bellows made themselves heard through the frantic music of the metropolis.

Then the agency sent her to do a fortnight's fill-in at the offices of *The New Technocrat*.

Molly had scarcely heard of, let alone read, this monthly journal and vaguely expected to find some small penny-pinching operation with a hand-cranked press. Instead, as she quickly realized, she was in the presence of influence, money, and a big circulation. *The New Technocrat* had been running for no more than a decade and its combination of financial, business and scientific expertise had made it a commercial winner.

Molly found herself seated at a desk and left with nothing to do for the first hour and a half. Then a stocky, smiling man in his thirties suddenly tossed some handwritten sheets before her and passed on without a word. She presumed they were meant for typing, but this proved no easy task as the handwriting was abominable and much of the language technical. When the man returned half an hour later and examined what little she had been able to do, he stopped smiling and enquired civilly if English were her second, or perhaps third, language. If she had not been too angry to articulate the reply which came bursting into her mind, that might have been an end of the matter. She had walked out of better offices than this. But instead of yelling, she beat out a rapid tattoo on the keys, tore off the sheet, and handed it to the man, who read it and then began smiling again.

So she made the acquaintance of Sam Keatley, Defence Correspondent of *The New Technocrat*. He was eleven years older than she was, amusing, considerate, mature, well paid without being rich, unambitious without being unexciting, friendly with everybody who mattered and related to nobody whether they mattered or not. He didn't play football, cricket, badminton, or tennis, and when he put his hand between her legs, he kept it there till the moment was ripe for a change of direction.

Six months later, they were married.

Eighteen months after that, they moved out to Westcliff-on-Sea.

And eight years after that one early September morning full of mist and promise Molly was washing the breakfast dishes when she heard her husband come home.

4

Molly sat on the edge of her armchair reluctant to surrender herself to comfort. The man from the Black Country had no such ambition but sank deeply into the sofa opposite her and ran his fingers appreciatively over the velvet dralon, leaving a track in the pile.

Aspinall was back in the kitchen, making the tea.

Sitting down seemed to have put the man in a better frame of mind, though he was still far from conciliatory.

'My name's Monk, missus,' he said. 'I'd like to get some things clear.'

'So would I,' said Molly in a high, strained voice. 'What you said about Sam, that was nonsense. Who are you? What's your authority?'

'Things you ought to understand,' continued Monk. 'You can ring the papers. They'll not print anything. You can ring the police. They'll not do anything. You can ring your solicitor. But all he'll do is tell you what I'm telling you and charge you a few bob for the telling.'

'What did you mean when you said Sam was a spy?' cried Molly. 'Please, that's ridiculous. This is a nightmare!'

'Do you know where he's gone?' asked Monk.

'No!'

'But you know he *has* gone. He must've said something.'

'Nothing. He said he was sorry.'

'What did he take?'

'I don't know. A little case. I don't know what was in it.'

'We'll have a look just now. You sure you didn't pack it for him, missus?'

'No. He just went off to the station like he usually does. Only, about twenty minutes later, he came back.'

Molly, having started to answer questions, was now gabbling

her replies as though after a certain number she would be guaranteed an explanation. The man frowned at her speculatively and put his finger through one of the unused buttonholes in his cardigan.

'Aspinall!' he bellowed.

The blond man appeared. He had taken the opportunity to repair his hair and the wave was back in full surge.

'It'll be a couple of minutes,' he said reproachfully.

'I hope you make a better cup of tea than you keep watch,' said Monk grimly. 'Tell us what happened.'

'You've seen Oakes?'

'We had a chat. Now I want to hear you.'

Aspinall glanced queryingly at Molly.

Monk said, 'Either she knows, or she'll have to know. Get on with it.'

'Well, we followed him to Southend station as usual. He parked the car and went into the station. Oakes followed. It was his turn. I waited till the train left, then set off back to town. They got me on the car-phone at Brentwood.'

'Oakes says he made a phone call in the station.'

'I didn't know that,' said Aspinall defensively. 'In any case, what difference would it have made?'

'To you, nought,' said Monk. 'He knows he's being watched. He tells his control. He's told to check back from the station this morning. They tell him to get out. So he steps off the train leaving Oakes stuck, waits till you've driven off, then comes on home for his bits and pieces. That the way of it, missus?'

'I don't know!' said Molly, very tense. 'I don't know *anything*. If you want me to know things, you'd better start telling me things. I don't feel like staying rational much longer.'

Monk nodded dismissively to Aspinall.

'Go and make that tea,' he said.

'I don't want any tea!' screamed Molly as the blond man left.

'All right, all right,' said Monk. 'Injured innocence, total surprise. It'll be hysterics next, so listen carefully and you needn't bother. Your hubby's an agent. It surprised us too, but we didn't have hysterics. We got his name from the Americans who got it from a KGB man called Leskov who defected in April last. You probably read about it. There might even have been a piece in *New Technocrat*, that'd be ironical. That's where you met him, wasn't it? You worked there.'

He said it so accusingly that she found herself shaking her head.

'Just for a fortnight. I went as a temp.'

'And ended up permanent. Or maybe not. So, Sam Keatley gets named. Daft, you think?'

'Insane,' said Molly emphatically.

'We checked it out, missus,' said Monk. 'We don't believe everything the KGB tells us. Or the Yanks either. On the surface there was nothing. Defence Correspondent, middle of the road politically, knock the government but didn't mind which government. Popular pieces in the dailies, right and left wing. Nothing controversial there, missus. Defence correspondents can't afford to be, else they don't get where they need to be. Sam Keatley rated top security clearance, but you'd know that. A safe man. Government research stations, scientific congresses abroad, NATO exercises, you could let Sam Keatley loose and rely on the results, just the scientific facts, no blurred moral edges. I'll tell you something that'll make you laugh, missus.'

'Bets?' said Molly.

'He looked so good, we tried to recruit him once! Can you imagine that? Just for debriefing after he'd been at any behind-the-curtain conferences. He must have been tempted. But he said no. He didn't want to compromise his journalistic reputation!'

'Let's get this straight,' said Molly. 'You're saying that my husband looks so innocent he must be guilty?'

Monk looked at her with the sadness of the man who's about to tell you that your house won't be finished for another three months.

'It works like that sometimes, missus,' he said. 'But no. We've watched him, photographed him, tapped his phone. We're sure.'

'Sure of what? That he went around snitching secrets from people's desks and selling them to the Russians? You must be crazy!'

'That's not as daft as it sounds either, missus,' said Monk seriously. 'Scientists can be pretty disorganized about where they put their stuff. Worse, they can be a bit mixed up about who should know what. Worst of all, they can even reckon it's their moral duty or whatever to pass what they know to their mates in Omsk. That's where your husband was really useful, missus. A sympathetic ear, knows his technical stuff, a good memory. I dare say that many a time there was nothing on paper. But it didn't really matter if there was. The Post Office would deliver it to the Embassy. Or he could take it direct. You know how many times he's been in the Eastern Bloc in the last two years alone? Eight!'

Aspinall came in with a tea tray.

'Three spoons for me,' said Monk.

'Mrs Keatley?' said Aspinall politely.

Molly felt very calm. The more detailed the account of Sam's alleged crimes became, the more manifestly absurd she knew it to be.

'If you believed this nonsense,' she said to Monk, 'why didn't you simply take my husband in for questioning? Why let this dangerous agent run loose?'

Monk helped himself to sugar and stood up with the teacup in his hand.

'You tell her, Aspinall,' he said. 'I'll have a poke around upstairs.'

He went out of the room.

'What's he mean?' demanded Molly.

'Well, to tell you the truth, your husband was more use to us loose than under wraps, Mrs Keatley,' said Aspinall almost apologetically. 'We really wanted to discover who his contacts were, find out where he was getting the stuff from. In fact if he hadn't got on to us and jumped off like he did, we'd probably not have bothered him, not for some time anyway. It would have made more sense just to feed him with duff stuff and waste a lot of their time.'

'I meant, what's he mean he's going to have a poke around,' interrupted Molly. 'Who the hell does he think he is? Excuse me.'

She found Monk sitting on the edge of her bed drinking his tea.

22

'You've got four rooms up here, haven't you, missus?' he said. 'Main bed, guest bed, one your husband used as an office, and a box room. How easy is it to get up to your attic?'

'You need a stepladder,' said Molly. 'What right have you got to come up here, Mr Monk?'

'The right of permission. Where do you keep the steps?'

'I gave you no permission,' said Molly.

'Oh yes you did. Aspinall heard you. Where did you say you kept the steps?'

'Under the stairs. I have given no permission for you to do anything in my house, Mr Monk. You may be able to interfere with newspapers printing and police investigating alleged espionage cases, but you won't stop them getting their teeth into assault and attempted rape.'

'Rape? Who's been raped?'

'Me. By you.'

'Don't talk daft, missus.'

'Not daft, Mr Monk. When I break that window and start shrieking, Aspinall will hear and people in the street will hear. And when they come to investigate they'll find me with my clothes torn and you with your face scratched.'

Monk considered for a moment.

'All right,' he said. 'I'm sorry if I seemed to be bullying you, missus. It was just a question of saving time and fuss. I thought we could just keep it among ourselves. But it'll be your fuss, not mine. Aspinall!'

'Yes,' came distantly from the lounge.

'I want a search warrant. And a WPC. Quick as you can,' he called, adding at normal level, 'She'll protect us both.'

'Hold on,' said Molly. 'What do you mean, fuss?'

'The more people outside the department who know about this, the wider the word'll spread. We can stop the papers printing details, but we can't stop news-items about a journalist going missing and we can't stop reporters pestering you for stories they hope to be able to print as soon as the gag's removed, and we can't stop other people getting in touch, relatives, friends, some not so friendly.'

'What are you trying to say, Mr Monk?' said Molly wearily.

'You help us, missus, we keep a low profile. You say you don't believe a word I say. But whatever you don't believe, you've got to admit your husband's up to something funny. So what's it to be? Truce, or do we start chatting to the neighbours?'

'That again,' said Molly, almost amused. 'At least you explain your threats a lot better than Mr Aspinall.'

Downstairs the phone rang.

They heard Aspinall pick it up, then he came trotting up the stairs.

'It's *The New Technocrat*,' he said. 'They want to know where their star reporter is.'

Monk looked at Molly but said nothing.

'What shall I do?' asked Molly.

'It's your phone, missus,' said Monk indifferently.

Molly sat on the bed and picked up the bedroom extension.

'Yes?' she said.

'Molly?'

She recognized the Scottish accent of Iain Haddon, the deputy editor.

'Hello, Iain,' she said.

'Where's that wild man of yours? He hasn't turned in yet. Did he sleep over, or something?'

'No, I'm sorry, Iain, I should 'ave rung earlier, but I was a bit preoccupied. Sam's a bit off-colour, I'm afraid.'

'Oh dear. I'm sorry to hear that. Nothing serious, I hope?'

'I don't think so. A virus or something.'

'Is he fit enough to have a wee word? Just for a second or two. I wouldn't ask, only there's a heap of things . . .'

'I'd rather not disturb him, Iain,' said Molly. 'He had a very restless night and the doctor's just been. That was him who answered the phone. He's dosed Sam and the poor dear's half way under now. I'm sorry.'

'Think nothing of it. It'll all keep. Get him on his feet soon, that's the main thing. Give him my love when he wakes up and tell him not to worry. I promise no one will do a stroke of his work! 'Bye, Molly.'

'Goodbye,' she said.

'That was very good,' said Monk regarding her speculatively. 'For someone who's had no experience, that was first class. Especially that touch about the doctor answering the phone.

That was really sharp, wasn't it, Aspinall?'

'Super,' said Aspinall. 'I'll get on with organizing the warrant now.'

'Don't be such a stumer!' said Monk. 'You'll find some steps under the stairs. Fetch them and have a crawl around the attic.'

Molly said, 'This is just till I've had time to think, you understand.'

Monk looked at her indifferently.

'Whatever you say, missus.'

5

Molly never let Monk out of her sight as he went round the house. Thoughts of planted evidence floated vaguely through her mind and though Aspinall could plant it just as easily, she had elected Monk the man most likely.

He seemed surprisingly familiar with the lay-out of the house.

'You know your way around,' she said accusingly.

'It's not Buckingham Palace, missus,' he replied.

They were in the study and he was going over Sam's desk like a waiter looking for a tip. In other circumstances such expertise might have been almost pleasurable to watch.

Molly sat in an old leather armchair with stuffing oozing out of a couple of gashes. Sam claimed it was the most comfortable seat in the house. It had been in his flat where they had lived for over a year after their marriage. Several times in those early days he had made love to her in this very chair, he sitting down, she kneeling astride. That was about as far as experimentation had taken them. Their enjoyment of each other had rarely seemed to need to be enhanced by quirks of venue or position.

In fact, she thought, altogether it had been a surprisingly conventional sort of marriage, even the age difference being about average for an office romance. Back home in Doncaster, her contemporaries had claimed to envy her lot; marriage to a journalist who sometimes appeared on the telly; a flat in central London; theatres, receptions, important people dropping in for cocktails. And in Doncaster Molly half believed it herself.

But it hadn't really been like that. Sam had turned out to be a real domestic animal and Molly was more than happy to let what remained of the 'sixties swing away without her. Even the famous 'central' flat was in reality nearer Ilford than the West End, and when Sam proposed a move, it was not towards the hub of things but out beyond the rim of West-cliff, hard by Southend. A friend in the office had inherited a house out there and decided to let rather than sell it, hoping (not without justice) that prices would rocket in the next decade. Sam expressed a desire to have a good garden and access to the sea, and even claimed the need to commute as an attraction, saying it put him out of easy reach and meant he could leave his work behind him at the end of the day.

So life for Molly had not been much different, she sometimes thought (with amusement, not regret), from what it might have been if she had married lanky, awkward, sports-obsessed Trevor and settled down in suburban Yorkshire.

And at least no one could ever have imagined *he* was a spy.

Except perhaps Monk.

He was crouched beneath the desk now, peering into the knee-hole and rapping on the woodwork like a ghost at a seance.

I'd better ask him a question, thought Molly almost light-heartedly. Memory of the simple *ordinariness* of her life with Sam had once again reassured her that this must all be some terrible, risible mistake.

'Mr Monk,' she said. 'According to your idea of things, where is Sam likely to be just now?'

His head rose above the desk top and his beady clerk's eyes regarded her unblinkingly.

'If you're wondering if we've got him or not, the answer's no, missus. They'd ring me here if they laid hands on him.'

'Then what, in terms of this lunatic plot of yours, do you personally, as an expert, imagine he's doing?' she asked with as much of a sneer as her unpractised face could manage.

'I'm not an imaginative man, missus,' said Monk. 'I just speculate on known facts and that's not always a help. You, for instance. I know all I *can* about you, missus, but I'm still not sure whether you're a very clever woman or a very stupid one. And that's a fact!'

'I just want to know that my husband's safe,' said Molly, feeling her light-hearted confidence ebb rapidly and tears begin to prick at her eyes. 'I just want to see him again and hear what he's got to say about this whole crazy business. Is *that* too stupid for you to understand?'

He stood up and shook his head. A noise that might have been a boss-shot at a laugh cracked from his mouth.

'For God's sake, missus, understand *this*. Your man's gone. He won't be coming back in a couple of weeks to sit and chat about things over a cup of cocoa. If you see him again in this country it'll be during visiting hours. But me, if you really want to know what I think, I think he's away. Not that that's going to do you any good. I think he's going sailing away. You're handy here for the river. All the big stuff coming down from Tilbury. I reckon he's sitting tightly curled in a stinking hold till some friendly freighter's got outside the limit. I'd get your fleecy boots out of mothballs, missus. The next time you're likely to see Sam Keatley, if you still want to see him that is, is in Moscow.'

She didn't believe it, tried to envisage it, saw a scene like a BBC set for *Uncle Vanya*, slid it from her mind like a holiday slide, got in its place a log cabin in a waste of snows, heard wolves howling distantly, felt Sam's hand on her shoulder, returned to here and now and realized that it was Monk patting her anxiously, comfortingly, and that the howl of the wolves was drifting up from the tundra of her own grief.

Fortunately Monk wasn't very good at comfort and her awareness of his ineptitude helped her to get a grip once more. But he was good at organizing and by the time she was back in the lounge drinking another cup of the much more naturally sympathetic Aspinall's strong sweet tea, her family doctor had been unearthed and peremptorily summoned.

She was angered by this interference in her affairs, but she realized there was no way of expressing her anger without its being interpreted as a symptom of her hysterical condition. Nor was she absolutely certain it wasn't. So she compromised, pretending to be worse than she felt but better than they feared. The tranquillizer that was prescribed was one she'd taken before, borrowed from a cheerfully neurotic friend who had observed her agitation before a visit to the dentist, so she knew and could cope with its relatively mild effect.

Under its calming effect, she realized that Monk was in a dilemma. He wanted to keep the story under wraps for the time being, but to do this he needed her co-operation. Molly suspected that the doctor had insisted that she must have company. The doctor's own discretion could be relied upon, but one confidante could lead to another, and the Keatleys' main circle of friends lay within the newspaper world. This, plus Molly's own antagonistic attitude, must have made the problem loom large.

He was helped, though he did not yet know it, by Molly's nature. She was not a secretive woman but she had inherited a strong sense of 'her own business' from her mother whose apparent garrulity revealed nothing she wanted to hide. In addition, her passionate belief in Sam's innocence needed the strong resistance of Monk's certainties to give it body and strength rather than the yielding shoulder of some uncritically sympathetic friend.

The problem was solved later in the day by the appearance of Iain and Jean Haddon.

The myth of Sam's illness could not be kept up for long at *The New Technocrat*, so Monk had grasped the nettle and, armed with a D-notice which made publication of material pertaining to the Keatley affair illegal, he had put the senior editorial staff on the journal into the picture. The Haddons were at precisely the degree of personal relationship with Molly that she needed at this moment. Jean was a sensible, bustling, down-to-earth Glaswegian woman whose company she enjoyed but rarely sought. Her husband was a bluff, shrewd Scot who managed to suppress but not altogether conceal the fact that his reaction to the affair was at least as strongly journalistic as personal.

They both expressed incredulity at the idea that Sam could be a foreign agent, but when Molly cited this as evidence to Monk, he sneered, 'Show me someone as does believe it straight off, missus, and I'll arrest him!'

No, thought Molly, sneered was not the right word. Monk's dismissal of any chance of official error about Sam's guilt was too absolute to need the underpinning of derision. In a curious way she came almost to enjoy the questioning sessions she underwent during the next few days, sometimes with Monk alone, sometimes with Aspinall present, sometimes with a couple of others. She answered all their questions frankly.

She had no doubt that, had she known where best to lie for Sam's sake, she would have lied. But she did not know, and her near-enjoyment derived from the fact that in nothing of what she told them so frankly could she see anything to support their accusations.

'I would have known!' she insisted savagely. 'He couldn't have hid so much for so long. I would have known.'

'Mebbe,' said Monk. And started again.

This went on for a week. Jean Haddon stayed with her during this time. To her other friends and neighbours Molly explained that Sam was on one of his fairly frequent trips abroad. The comings and goings at the house probably aroused curiosity, but nothing, as she explained to Jean, which the neighbours would not put down to a sudden outburst of sub-urban nymphomania.

The only trace of Sam had been the discovery of the Datsun in a multi-storey car park near Tilbury. The car was being examined by forensic experts, Monk told her. Molly pressed him close, both fearing and hoping that this meant there were bloodstains, signs of a struggle. He shook his head.

'No, missus. Wherever he's gone, he wasn't forced.'

'Except by you bastards,' snapped Molly and slammed the door as she left the room.

Generally, however, she kept her feelings well under control during the day, though the nights were a different matter. If she tried to rest without her tranquillizer her mind slowly filled with strange floating shapes which arranged themselves finally into some surrealist parody of the bulbous towers of Moscow blurred by a net of swirling snow which caught her heart so icily that she would wake up shivering and weeping in the heated bedroom.

Jean Haddon wanted her to go and stay at her house in Middlesex, but Molly was reluctant. She felt instinctively that she must not relinquish any more control of her actions unless she wished to relinquish all.

Then one night the phone rang.

'Molly?' It was her mother's voice. She could have wept to hear that familiar, bossy Yorkshire intonation. It was the knowledge that she almost certainly would have wept that had prevented her making any contact herself.

'Hello, Mum,' she said.

'We haven't heard from you for over a week,' said Mrs Haddington accusingly.

'I know. I'm sorry. I've been . . . busy.'

'Too busy for your own? Well, you must've been busy then. I just wanted to be sure about Friday.'

'Friday?'

'Aye. You and Sam are coming for the weekend. You've not forgot?'

She had, of course. Just as she'd forgotten a dinner engagement two nights earlier and indeed every plan she and Sam had made for the shaken future.

'Oh, Mum, I'm sorry. Sam's away, he had to go abroad unexpectedly and he won't be back.'

She almost choked on the unintended irony of the lie. There was a disapproving (disappointed?) snort down the receiver.

'Does that mean you're not coming then? Your dad's been fair looking forward to it.'

Her mother would never admit directly to her own disappointment. Suddenly Molly heard herself saying, 'No, what I thought was, Mum, I'd come up by myself and with Sam being away, I can maybe stay a few days longer, if that's OK?'

'Of course it's OK. It's your home isn't it? Grand. Will you be driving up?'

'No. I'll come by train. That one that gets in about four.'

'That's good. I don't like you on the road without Sam. I'll meet you at the station. Take care.'

Jean Haddon thought it was an excellent idea. Molly didn't blame her for her enthusiasm. A week was quite long enough to be stuck in a strange house with a neurotic woman.

When she told Monk of her decision, he gave her a long assessing look.

'Might as well, missus,' he said finally. 'You look a bit done in and being up there'll give you a bit more time when the news breaks and the reporters start yapping around down here.'

'The news breaks?' she echoed in alarm. 'Has something happened? What . . .'

'No, no, no,' he said impatiently. 'Not from us. We're still keeping it quiet. Not for your sake, you understand that, missus. I won't fool you. No, there's always a chance some of your husband's contacts might still not know what's going on and show themselves.'

'If there *are* any contacts!' snapped Molly.

Monk ignored her, reducing her protest to a mere token. Was it anything else now? she wondered.

'No,' he proceeded. 'It'll be the Russians who go for the headlines when he gets to Moscow.'

'But you said he was probably on his way a week ago!' said Molly, triumphant as a debater making a sharp point.

'It wouldn't be the QE2 he's travelling on, missus,' answered Monk reasonably. 'And when he gets there, they'll mebbe bide their time. They like to pick their moment, make the most of it. For instance, there's a big get-together next month to decide whether NATO should buy the British or the American radar-scrambler. You've likely read about it. The Russians would love to produce the Defence Correspondent of *The New Technocrat* the day before, dropping large hints that what he doesn't know about both devices isn't worth giving to the Chinese. That's how they work.'

He sounded positively admiring.

'We'll see,' was the best Molly could manage.

'We will,' he agreed. 'So you go off and build up your strength. We've done with you for the moment, I think. Anyway, you'll be leaving us your address.'

'I suppose you'll be keeping an eye on me,' said Molly sarcastically as Monk rose to leave.

He didn't answer till he was on the doorstep.

'If we do, you'll not notice, missus,' he said. 'Not unless you've been trained to notice, that is. Have a nice trip.'

She watched him go. A neighbour's curtain twitched. Did they think Monk was her fancy man?

Or perhaps she was under observation already.

She was suddenly desperately homesick for Doncaster.

6

Molly's mother was waiting by the ticket barrier at the station. She looked rather pale and tired but this was not uncommon. Mrs Haddington did everything to the full limits of her energy. Including talking.

'Hello, love,' she said. 'Nice journey? You look a bit thinner. You've not been on that diet again? I've had such a rush. I've been to the British Home Stores for a bit of cheese for your dad's Welsh Rabbit and you should have seen the queue. What's the weather been like down there?'

'We've had a lot of rain,' said Molly.

'Don't talk to me about rain! You should have been here last Tuesday. I've never seen rain like it. What are you doing?'

Molly had stopped outside the station by the empty taxi rank.

'There'll be one along in a minute,' she said.

'You're never getting a taxi! Do you know how much they charge now? It's only a step to the bus stop and it takes you near on up to the door. I walked it just the other week. There's a lot of life in these old legs yet!'

'It's not your old legs I'm worried about,' said Molly, pointing at her two cases. 'It's my old arms. You walk if you like. I'm riding! How's Dad?'

'Same as always. His sciatica bothers him more than he lets on, but he doesn't say much. He's due to retire this year and he's trying to wangle to stay on a bit. He'd be lost at home. But if they think he's not fit, there's no chance so he says.'

Molly sat in the taxi that arrived soon after and listened happily to her mother's unceasing flow of chatter, more than content to play a minor tributary role. She had had enough of being the centre of things.

'How much did he charge you? And you gave him a tip! He didn't even carry your cases up to the door!' said Mrs Haddington indignantly as she looked for her key.

'It's not exactly a long drive,' said Molly, looking at the dozen feet of path that lay between the door and the gate of the terraced house in which she had been born and raised. It was an important distance, however, as she came to realize as she grew older, putting their terrace several classes above those fronting directly on to the pavement. For all that, these houses in the older suburbs seemed to be slipping irretrievably down-market aided by the desire of agents and mortgage companies to push the modern boxes mushrooming on outlying estates. But the boom in house prices and in the cost of petrol had reawoken the bourgeoisie to the advantages of solid-built older property within easy reach of the town centre and there was nothing down-market about Rothwell Avenue now.

'Old Mrs Turncott in twenty-three died,' said Mrs Haddington, opening the door. 'There's a pair of schoolteachers in there now. Paid near on nine thousand, I heard. Danny! Danny-boy! Look who's here!'

A huge dog, half Labrador, half Alsatian, came galloping down the narrow hallway and lashed Molly's face with his tongue.

'Down Danny! Danny-boy, get down!' ordered Molly. The dog paid no heed and she had to lean all her weight on his collar to get him to the floor. Sam had opined that Danny ought to be put into stationary orbit above the RSPCA headquarters so he could crap on the officials of that organization evermore. Danny, with the altruistic love of a missionary, always made a vast fuss of Sam who, after only a token resistance, allowed himself to be converted into an enthusiastic dog-walker whenever they visited Doncaster. Molly recalled this now and was glad that Danny-boy's tongue gave her an excuse to wipe her face.

'He's that excited at seeing you,' said Mrs Haddington. 'Let's have a cup of tea, love. How long are you going to be able to stay? I hate these short visits!'

'When are you going back?' asked her father shortly after his

34

arrival home from work. He wasn't being unwelcoming. On the contrary. So precious did he count the minutes of Molly's visits – or indeed any period of pleasure – that he was hyper-sensitive to the speed at which they trickled away. All her stays at home since she went to work in London had been punctuated with heavy sighs and 'This time next week – next Tuesday – tomorrow – you'll be gone.'

All of which Molly found both touching and amusing, remembering how, as a teenager, her friends, her hours and her clothes had been a constant distress to him. His intoler-ance had been matched by her own, and at fifteen she had been quite in accord with his sternly expressed judgement that the sooner they were shot of her, the better.

Now he sat and regarded her anxiously from his straight-backed uncomfortable armchair, a short squat man who even when (or perhaps especially when) freshly scrubbed seemed to have on him a patina of the red dust from the brickyard where he had been foreman for the past twenty years. He had come home, got cleaned up, had his tea and was now smoking the first of three Park Drive. When he'd finished these he would rise, put on the jacket of the dark blue suit whose trousers he'd changed into before tea, and take Danny for a walk. On his return he would smoke another couple of cigar-ettes, then announce, as though the idea had just blossomed in his mind for the first time ever, that he might just pop down to the Club. Mrs Haddington possessed the right of veto, though not more than twice in a week and never on Fridays and Saturdays, when she possessed the right of inclu-sion.

And though Molly's father had grown more and more en-thusiastic about her visits as the years went by, he never saw much reason to let them interfere with the old-established pattern of his existence.

'I'm staying a week, maybe longer,' said Molly.

'Is Sam not coming then?'

'Sam's away. Don't you ever listen?' interrupted her mother.

Ivor Haddington mused through his second cigarette.

'You won't know when you're going back then?' he said finally.

'Are you wanting rid of me, Dad?' asked Molly, smiling at her mother.

'No. Of course not. I just like to know where I am.'

'It's his social engagement book. It gets so full of garden parties and the like,' observed Mrs Haddington, beginning to clear the table. 'No, you sit still, love. First night home.'

She bustled out of the room with a perilous pile of dishes.

'What's she on about, garden parties?' wondered her husband.

'Joke, Dad.'

'She'll be getting up on amateur night next.'

They sat in silence till the third fag was finished. Danny, lying quietly under the table, jumped up and barked as soon as the butt was flicked into the fire. Mr Haddington regarded him for a puzzled moment, then said, 'I might just take the old dog for a walk.'

He stood up and unhooked his jacket from the back of one of the dining chairs. As he put it on, Molly was suddenly reminded of the crumpled suit that Monk had worn every time she saw him.

Jumping up, she said, 'I think I'll come with you, Dad. I'd like a bit of exercise.'

'Oh ay? All right,' said Haddington with no overt enthusiasm.

They kept Danny on the leash for the first twenty minutes till they reached the Town Field, several acres of open grassland mainly given over to various kinds of sports fields. Here they let the dog loose and followed him slowly across the damp grass as he gambolled off into mist-accelerated dusk.

'Everything all right?' said her father suddenly.

'Yes, of course. Why?'

'Nowt. Just so's I know.'

Molly was taken aback. It would be ironic if her father had guessed at some trouble as one of the reasons for coming out on the walk had been to avoid the oblique interrogation her mother always subjected her to on the first evening home. It usually concerned her plans for having a family and the future of Sam's job. Molly could understand her interest in the first of these and had assured her on several occasions that she and Sam did nothing to prevent pregnancy but so far they had just been unlucky.

Or perhaps, as things turned out, lucky.

Since her thirty-third birthday, her attitude had been less casual. It seemed a significant advance, even more than thirty. A century's first riding. She had talked with her doctor, had tests. There was no reason why she could not have a child. Sam had expressed delight when she told him, been tested himself, was all right, all that was needed was constant application he assured her and for a couple of weeks that was what she got. Then had come this period of self-distancing and loss of sexual appetite. He claimed he was working too hard. Certainly he seemed to be keeping longer hours than usual. They had made love only once in the week before his departure. The thought had crossed her mind that he might be having an affair, but she dismissed it as impossible till Monk's visit had brought it back as a flimsy but desirable lifeline.

Perhaps her mother's mind had moved in that direction too. Her interest in Sam's job had always been ambivalent. She was proud of his importance as evidenced by the places he visited and the people he met, but she didn't really approve of his spending so much time away from home. Mrs Haddington liked Sam – he was an easy person to like – and perhaps this intermittent friendship had enabled her to sense something not quite sound in his life, something which had been merely subsumed into the background of Molly's much more intimate relationship.

I'm beginning to believe it, thought Molly. Deep inside I'm beginning to accept all that Monk has told me.

'Your mam's been poorly lately, did she tell you?' said Ivor abruptly.

'No, she didn't. What's been the matter?'

'I don't know. We had the quack. Then she had some tests.'

Molly found it momentarily difficult to focus on any cause for concern other than Sam. She almost resented having to.

'Tests? What sort of tests? Why didn't anyone tell me?'

She knew it was pretty hopeless expecting details from Ivor, who regarded medicine with a superstitious hatred and fear, and reckoned ignorance preferable to any diagnosis.

'You know what she's like. Says you'll have worries enough of your own without adding to them. She's got some pills and seems a lot better now, so happen she's right.'

'So why're you telling me now, Dad?'

'I don't rightly know,' said Mr Haddington. 'I don't like secrets in a family, that's all. There's always bother later. *You should've told me, you should've said.* And the real trouble can, like, get lost. Danny! Danny! Where's the silly bugger got to?'

It was getting quite dark now. The kids playing football had reluctantly conceded defeat. On the distant road car lights floated through the rising autumn mist.

'Danny!' called Molly. 'Danny-boy! Come!'

There was a joyful bark and then the great dog came lolloping towards them.

'Ay. He'll come for you,' grunted Haddington, looking at his watch. 'We'd best be getting back. I've a snooker match tonight. Win this and I'll be through to semis.'

'Why don't you go straight to the Club, Dad, and get a bit of practice?' suggested Molly. 'I'll take Danny home. I'm enjoying the walk and he won't mind.'

'No. He'd walk all night if you'd a mind to let him,' said Haddington. He hesitated, then added, 'It'd be handy. The fellow I'm playing's on the dole. He'll have been practising since tea-time. You sure you'll be all right?'

Molly laughed. 'You're not worried I'll get lost, are you?'

'No. But there's some funny buggers hang about the Field. A girl got attacked just the other week.'

'I can look after myself, Dad. Down in London we're being attacked all the time, that's what you used to think, wasn't it? And besides, it'd take a brave man to chance his arm against Danny.'

'Him! He's a big soft nowt,' said Haddington. 'But he looks vicious, right enough. All right then. Thanks, love.'

He turned and strode off into the darkness, then stopped and came back.

'Tell your mother I left you on the road, will you?' he said.

'Oh get on!' said Molly. 'And make sure you win!'

He walked stiffly away. His sciatica must be bothering him

but it would be a point of honour with him not to show it. Or perhaps 'honour' placed it too high, socially speaking. Honour was a toffee-nosed way of advertising your superiority without boasting. Sam had said that, perhaps the nearest thing to a radical statement he had ever made. Don't think about Sam. Men like Ivor Haddington had no truck with honour. They knew that pain must be tholed. It was the lesson of their history, and not one that a car, a fridge and the NHS could help them unlearn, any more than death duties and supertax could undo the damage of a thousand years of Norman blood.

Was that a radical thought or a reactionary one? she wondered. Just as some people have no sense of how to hit a moving ball, so she had no sense of politics. She was neither proud nor ashamed of her class. She voted Labour because her father had taught her there was no other way to vote, but was bewildered when she read of Labour politicians talking about each other in terms which she had thought were exclusively reserved for Tories. Sam, himself studious to avoid any extreme position in discussions with their friends, had seemed almost possessively proud of her political naïvety and would trot it out to cool any overheating debate.

But she had been able to thrash him at tennis.

She was thinking about Sam again. She didn't want to think about him any more, not until she knew *how* to think about him. Irritatedly she looked around for Danny. He was nowhere in sight. In fact very little was except the distant glow of lights along the road. He had shown some uncertainty when her father had walked away. Perhaps he had gone in pursuit. But Ivor Haddington would have sent or brought him back.

Something moved, perhaps a hundred yards away, a shape dark against the darkness and substantial in the swirling mist.

'Danny?' she called. 'Danny-boy! Here boy!'

The shape was not Danny, she knew that. Nor was it simply another pedestrian traversing Town Field. The mist swirled and hardened the outline for a second; broad-brimmed hat, belted coat, like a Gestapo agent in an old war movie she thought, but she could not make herself smile at the thought;

39

it stood there, vague again, quite still, watching, listening. Waiting? She turned and began to walk hurriedly towards the smear of light which was the road. Fear was like a fishbone in her throat. Her breathing was fast and shallow. The chill night air was clammy against her flushed and burning skin. In her mouth too it felt more liquid than gaseous. It condensed on her tongue, her gullet, her lungs. She was drowning above ground. Behind her there was sudden violent movement, the menacing rush of feet. She turned, not bravely but in despair, for the terror of not turning is in the end the greatest terror.

And Danny barked joyously at having sneaked up on her and taken her so completely by surprise.

Close by a couple strolled with a Cairn terrier which whispered threats deep in its throat at Danny. There was hardly any mist at all. Three young boys were breaking the law by cycling over the grass about fifty yards away. There was nothing which remotely resembled a menacing watching figure.

But she slipped the leash on to Danny's collar before she resumed her progress to the lighted road.

7

'There's Trevor and his wife,' said Mrs Haddington. They were sitting drinking coffee in the restaurant of Doncaster's largest store. It shared a floor with the furniture department and Molly looked up to see her erstwhile fiancé and his wife examining a three-piece suite.

'I think she's pregnant again,' said Mrs Haddington.

'Who needs toads?' said Molly. 'How many will that be?'

'Just three. They've got a house in Sprotbrough now. He's done very well.'

Sprotbrough was a 'desirable dormer village' (according to the estate agents) on the other side of the by-pass. A bourgeois battery. Had Sam said that? Or was it in fact Trevor when his sights had been set on the luxury apartment in Brussels?

Perhaps her defection (Christ! that word) had taken some of the steam out of him. No, she was flattering herself. What was Westcliff-on-Sea but one of London's many Sprotbroughs and she'd taken to life there like a duck to water. Or a hen to a battery. Except that there were no chicks. Thank God, thank God.

'I never cared for her,' said Mrs Haddington. 'She's very effective.'

'Affected,' said Molly.

'I knew her mother. She was a Ramsey. A nice enough woman, but common. They had a caravan after the war. Up Scawsby way before they built the estate.'

'She's all right, Jennifer,' said Molly.

'All right for breeding,' said her mother. 'The Ramseys were always good at that.'

She was getting ready to mount an attack, thought Molly. The previous night Molly had fended off her tentative probings by launching a series of counter-enquiries about her mother's health. She had gained no ground but a temporary truce had

41

been established and they had watched television and talked on neutral topics till Ivor had come home flushed with ale and victory.

But now the occasion of the attack looked like being its interrupter, for the Challengers had come into the restaurant area and were looking around hopelessly for a free table in the Saturday morning crowd when Jennifer's gaze met Molly's. She smiled with the exaggerated delight with which she always greeted her predecessor in Trevor's affections and headed towards Molly's table. Her husband followed with less overt enthusiasm.

'Hello, Molly. Hello, Mrs Haddington. Do you mind if we join you?'

'Sit down,' said Mrs Haddington. 'We'll be going just now.'

'Hello, Molly,' said Trevor.

She looked at him with more coldness than she intended and his social smile began to fade. They had met only infrequently and briefly in the past twelve years, usually such accidental encounters as this. Sam had, gleefully, forced her to introduce him on one occasion and had surprised her later by remarking, apparently sincerely, what a good-looking man Trevor was. To Molly his features had never really lost that not-quite-formed look which is fine at nineteen but hints some deficiency at thirty. Today, for the first time almost, she saw him as his age. Her age. He regarded her warily. Hauntedly almost? Who was she to read faces?

At last she remembered to smile.

'Sam not here, Molly?' enquired Jennifer, whose small pert face was rendered almost doll-like by a mask of make-up. Hides the swarthy skin, opined Mrs Haddington. She might be right there, but Molly could see no outer evidence of pregnancy.

'No, he's off on a trip,' said Molly.

'They have all the fun,' said Jennifer. 'Trevor's just back from Scotland, aren't you, dear?'

'I'd hardly call Glasgow fun,' said Trevor.

'I hear you've moved to Sprotbrough,' said Molly.

'Yes. Well, it made sense to move to a bigger house with the family growing up,' said Jennifer.

'And another one on the way, dear?' said Mrs Haddington.

'There's no hiding things from you, Mrs Haddington,' said Jennifer, visibly annoyed.

'It's not a secret, is it? I'm sorry, I didn't realize,' said Mrs Haddington in spuriously apologetic tones. Molly caught Trevor's eye and for a second they shared amusement.

'Oh no,' said Jennifer sweetly. 'It's the third, after all. You don't make a secret of the *third*, do you?'

'Well, best get on with shopping,' said Mrs Haddington abruptly. 'Come on, Molly. *Molly!*'

'Sorry,' said Molly. She had been looking idly round the restaurant. At a table against the wall at the far side was a man reading a newspaper. All she could see over the top of it was a wave of blond hair but it had been no surprise when the paper was slowly lowered to reveal Aspinall.

He returned her gaze, then folded his paper, stood up and walked slowly into the furnishing department where he began to look at a mahogany wardrobe.

Mrs Haddington was on her feet.

'Nice to see you again, Molly,' said Trevor.

'Yes. Do come round and have a coffee one day if you get fed up of being by yourself,' said Jennifer. 'Our new address is in the phone book.'

'She must put that stuff on with a putty knife,' observed Mrs Haddington as they approached the stairs. 'They always had bad complexions, the Ramseys. Swarthy.'

'They seem happy,' said Molly.

'*Seem*,' said Mrs Haddington significantly. 'I've heard that there's been goings-on. Not that I pay any heed. You know what Sprotbrough's like for gossip.'

'Oh Mum!' said Molly. 'Look, I think I've left a glove. I'll catch you up in a minute downstairs.'

She turned and retraced her steps. Aspinall had turned his attention to a double bed with a Union Jack continental quilt. She walked straight up to him. He smiled amiably at her.

'Hello, Mrs Keatley,' he said.

'What the hell are you doing here?' she demanded without preamble. 'Is this Monk's idea of discreet surveillance?'

'Oh no!' he said, shocked. 'You don't think you're being watched, do you?'

'I'm ready to think anything,' she said. 'What are you playing at then?'

'I just wanted a quick word and I didn't want to approach you while you were with your mother. You haven't told her anything, I take it?'

'What do I know to tell her?' asked Molly. 'But she'll be looking for me in a moment. What is it you want? Have you got some news of Sam?'

Aspinall shook his head.

'It's just that Mr Monk would like a word with you.'

'Couldn't he just telephone?'

Aspinall shrugged.

'He wanted a personal chat. Can you get away tonight for a few minutes?'

Molly considered. It seemed absurd that she should let herself get involved with such cloak-and-dagger stuff, but on the other hand if Monk thought it important enough to come to Doncaster to see her, it might be worth her while to co-operate.

'I'll take our dog out for a walk,' she said. 'About eight o'clock. On the Town Field. You can tell him where that is, I dare say, Mr Aspinall.'

She observed him closely but he showed no reaction to the innuendo.

'I can find out,' he said. 'Thanks, Mrs Keatley. I'm sorry to have troubled you.'

'Sir, madam, can I help you?'

It was a smiling salesman who pressed one hand down upon the mattress as he spoke as though limbering up for his sales pitch.

'Oh no,' said Molly. 'We're just looking.'

She turned away from the professional smile and across the breadth of the furniture department she had a glimpse of Trevor and Jennifer Challenger staring at her from the restaurant. Their heads turned away instantly.

'Excuse me,' she said to Aspinall and strode off to join her mother.

✻

After lunch, Mrs Haddington said, 'I've put a fire on in the front room.'

This meant that the living-room, where they had just eaten the steak and kidney pie which was served at one p.m. prompt every Saturday, was now the exclusive domain of Ivor, who would watch the sports programme for ten minutes and then fall asleep.

'It's nice to see a coal fire,' said Molly sinking on to the sofa. The room had hardly changed since the days when she and Trevor used to curl up here, she full of romance, he full of lust.

'Yes. Better for you than just that central heating,' said Mrs Haddington, looking with scornful pride at the radiator which Sam and Molly had paid for a couple of years earlier. 'There's nowt like a coal fire in your own home. Excuse me a moment, love.'

Something in her mother's voice caught Molly's attention, but she felt too drowsily comfortable to analyse what it was. She wasn't used to eating so much in the middle of the day and before the meal her mother had produced the bottle of Dubonnet she got specially for her daughter's visits.

Molly closed her eyes for a moment and when she opened them again, nearly an hour had passed and the fire needed mending. Nor had her mother appeared.

Molly went out into the kitchen but it was empty. In the living-room a horse race was driving a TV commentator into a state of hysterical incoherence without disturbing Mr Haddington's slumbers. Molly closed the door quietly and went upstairs.

She found her mother sitting on the edge of her bed. She had clearly been lying down and Molly guessed that she had pushed herself upright as she heard her daughter's approach.

'Hello, dear. I felt so sleepy I just had a little nap,' she said.

Molly looked closely at her face which was pale and drawn, then at the bedside table which bore a tumbler and a bottle of pills.

'What are you taking, Mum?' she asked.

'Oh, nothing. Something for my back. I get a bit of backache sometimes and the doctor gave me these.'

Molly squinted at the label which was as illegible as such things traditionally are, then took out a pill and examined it. There was a trade-name on it and she mouthed it carefully.

'Don't make me have to go to a chemist and ask what these things are for, Mum,' she said.

Her mother stood up and started busying herself at the dressing-table. At first Molly felt irritated, thinking this was just another manifestation of the obduracy which always characterized her mother's approach to matters she considered her own affair and no one else's.

'For God's sake, Mum . . .' began Molly, then she glimpsed the face reflected in the dressing-table mirror and to her horror, instead of the expected mind-your-own-business expression, she saw that her mother was crying.

'Mum, please, don't, what is it?'

She felt completely at a loss. They had always been pretty close, got on pretty well, but this role was one which their relationship had never ever permitted her even to imagine. Her mother's very real concern for Molly's well-being had somehow stopped short of actually mothering. They were not a kissing, hugging, embracing kind of family and even now as, full of anxiety, Molly put her arm around her mother's shoulder, she was able to appreciate (and be angry at) the unfamiliar awkwardness of the gesture.

'Mum, please, what is it?' she repeated.

'It's nothing. I'm being daft. It's a sign of age. It's just that sometimes I let myself get to thinking,' said Mrs Haddington. She had allowed herself to be eased down on to the bed, but now she stood up abruptly so that she broke free of Molly's embrace.

'I'm all right as long as I'm doing things,' she said. 'Don't let on to your dad you've seen me like this.'

'Mum, what is the matter with you?' demanded Molly, angry now. 'Either tell me or I'll ring Dr Lamb this minute.'

'No need for that,' said her mother. 'I'm going to see him Monday morning. You can come along if you've nothing better to do.'

This invitation frightened Molly more than anything else. Her mother had always hated it to be known that she was visiting either her doctor or dentist. Old acquaintances met in the waiting-room were greeted with the most distant of nods and attempts at conversation were icily ignored. For Mrs Haddington to invite company, however half-heartedly, meant she was afraid.

'But you just saw the doctor a couple of days ago. Dad told me. Why do you have to go back?'

'Your dad talks too much,' said Mrs Haddington disapprovingly. 'I told him to say nowt. Anyway he only knows the part of it.'

Molly groaned.

'Mum,' she said. 'Am I going to be let into the big secret, or not?'

'There's no secret. I just don't like to worry people. There's no need to run to meet trouble. But as you're here, you might as well know. I started bleeding a while back.'

'Bleeding?'

'That's right. You know, bleeding,' said her mother, powdering her face vigorously. 'At first I thought it was the curse come back. But I'd been done with that long enough and I got to worrying. You read things. They put everything in magazines these days. So I went to see Dr Lamb.'

'Did Dad go with you?' asked Molly, half ironically.

'Oh no. He didn't know I'd gone. But then I had to go into hospital for the day on Wednesday and I had to tell him, as I didn't know if I'd be back to make his tea. But I just let on I was going to see Dr Lamb. You know what your dad's like about hospitals.'

'What did you have to go to the hospital for?' demanded Molly.

'Tests,' said Mrs Haddington airily. 'Just having an examination.'

'You mean a d. and c.?' said Molly. 'A dilatation and currettage? They scraped you?'

'Yes,' said Mrs Haddington, looking slightly annoyed as if her thunder had been stolen. 'Well, I said nothing to your dad. You'd rung the night before, remember, and said you'd like to come up on Friday. And I was going in to see Dr Lamb on Friday morning for the results.'

'What did he say, Mum?' asked Molly anxiously.

'Nothing. There'd been some delay or a mix-up. They

weren't ready. So I've to go back on Monday.'

'That bloody hospital!' said Molly angrily, recalling her mother's pale and strained face at the station. 'And what about these pills?'

'They're just for my nerves,' said Mrs Haddington. 'Not that they're much use. I took one before and you saw what it did to me!'

'Why didn't you tell me all this yesterday?' asked Molly.

'And spoil your visit straight off? Besides, what's to tell? It could all be nothing in the end. Is that the time? I'd better start thinking about the tea!'

Mrs Haddington bustled out of the room, leaving Molly staring helplessly into the mirror. It could all be nothing in the end! Was there any terror human beings couldn't conjure out of existence?

For the second time that afternoon the face she saw in the dressing-table glass was streaked with tears.

8

At eight o'clock, Molly was walking slowly across Town Field with Danny bounding ecstatically alongside. She had persuaded her parents to go to the Club for the usual Saturday night show, promising she herself would look in later for a drink. Her mother had started to protest, but Molly had insisted and in the end Mrs Haddington had looked at Ivor and nodded significantly as though acceding to a threat.

Somehow the knowledge of her mother's fear of cancer permitted Molly to think more clearly about Sam than at any time since his disappearance nearly a fortnight earlier, almost as if now at last she had something to test the pain of his loss against. The loss, she told herself coldly, could possibly be as absolute as death with Sam gone beyond recall, beyond encounter, ever again. But that was absurd. Suppose he did end up in Moscow? There were package tours to Russia these days. She knew several people who had gone off for three or four days at Easter and come back as Soviet experts for evermore. If she knew where Sam was, then the possibility of seeing him again was there. No, not possibility. She *must* see him again. But her heart filled with fear at the prospect.

Suppose I'm faced with the choice? Life alone in England. Life with Sam in Russia.

If that ever becomes a choice, then Sam *is* a traitor. What's a traitor? Do I care that my country has been deceived, cheated, sold?

Sold. What could he possibly have got out of it? There'd been no sign of any hidden source of income. Sam's salary had been good, kept them comfortable, but there'd been little left over for extravagances. They lived well, but not luxuriously. He never grudged money. They had put central heating and the telephone in her parents' house, for instance. But he had been a strict though democratic overseer of household expenditure. Perhaps his extra-curricular earnings had all gone into the Co-op Bank in Moscow. Perhaps he was a rouble millionaire.

In her new mood of clarity she acknowledged fully for the first time that, whatever happened, her life was altered beyond repair. She had tired her mind in working out explanations of Sam's behaviour which posited his innocence. But as far as his relationship with herself went, even the simplest of these involved him in deceits almost as great as those of his guilt.

This was what clarity of mind brought you to. She could imagine scenarios in which Sam would not have cheated his country but none in which he would not have cheated her.

'Evening, missus,' said Monk. 'You'd best look where you're going or you'll walk into a goal post.'

He was walking close by her side, matching step for step, with Danny at his heel giving every appearance of welcoming an old and respected acquaintance.

Molly looked round in surprise and saw that she must indeed have covered a couple of hundred yards quite oblivious of her surroundings. The night was much clearer than the previous one and she could make out all the perimeters of the field. She was three-quarters of the way across and heading towards the leisure centre which had grown up on the western flank.

'Have you got any news of Sam?' she asked.

He shook his head. He was wearing an officer's riding mac. On another man it might have been an affectation of gentility. On him the ill-fitting and soiled garment looked like a trophy. She had no doubt that the blue suit was crushed beneath it.

'Not a word,' he said. 'There was a Rumanian cargo ship, seemed a likely bet. But it had trouble.'

Fire. Collision. Sam trapped like a rat in the hold.

Monk shook his head again as though catching her thought.

'Engine trouble,' he said. 'Had to put in at Athens. Greek Customs went aboard and kept their eyes skinned, just as a favour. But all he needs is a leather cap and a sou'-wester and who's to tell the difference?'

'Why are you telling me this?' she asked.

'To explain the delay,' he said, surprised. 'We'd have expected him to show by now. Not officially, not publicly. There's others as will time that for him. But to show so that we'd know he's got there.'

His choice of terms fitted one of Molly's innocence theories and, halting so suddenly that Danny ran into them, she asked Monk, 'Sam's not working for you, is he, Mr Monk? This isn't just a plant, what do you call it, some sort of double agent?'

He turned and faced her. She hated the expression of near sympathy which skimmed across his shrewd clerk's face.

'No, missus,' he said. 'He's not one of ours. Sorry.'

'You'd have to say that,' she retorted.

'I'd have to say it,' he agreed. 'That's the funny thing about my job, missus. The lies and the truth are nearly always the same. It's handy. You don't have to think.'

'Then it doesn't matter what I think, does it?' she flashed at him. 'Why shouldn't I choose what gives me most comfort?'

They resumed walking.

'That's up to you,' he said indifferently.

'Why did you ask to meet me, Mr Monk?'

'Partly to reassure you, missus. I know you'll be worried.'

'That's kind,' she mocked. 'But couldn't Goldilocks have done that?'

'Who? Aspinall? I dare say. But it wasn't just kind. We wouldn't want you getting overwrought, doing anything that might stir things up.'

'That sounds more like it.'

'You'd let us know if anyone tried to get in touch with you, Mrs Keatley?'

'Would I? Who, for instance? And wouldn't you know, anyway? With your tapped telephones and watchers in the shadows?'

'You've been dipping in the wrong books, missus,' said Monk. 'We don't have them sort of powers or that sort of manpower. Not without a lot of bother anyway.'

'Oh come on!' said Molly. 'Don't pretend you're not having me watched. Aspinall this morning. The Boston strangler last night.'

'Who?'

'That fellow who was hanging around when I brought the dog over here last night. I'd get rid of him. He couldn't keep out of sight in a fog!'

Monk frowned and shook his head but didn't say anything. They were almost at the edge of the grass and they halted again by the path that ran between the two main buildings of the leisure centre.

'Is that all, Mr Monk?' enquired Molly.

Monk shook his head.

'Just a couple of things, missus. You know a woman called Hibbert? Sally Ann Hibbert?'

'No.'

'Your husband never mentioned her?'

'No. Why?'

'She's an American. She spent a year at Durham while your husband was there in the 'fifties.'

'A lot of people did.'

'They knew each other well.'

'Go on!' said Molly. 'I bet they used to clench their fists together at CP meetings.'

She listened to herself uneasily. Monk brought out something new in her, a kind of bitchy cynicism which she'd always deprecated in other women. She longed for the cosy housewife she used to be, but even as she longed, she wondered why Sam had been so content with a cosy housewife.

'CP,' said Monk. 'Interesting you should say that.'

'Why? Is it true?'

'No. Just interesting. They both floated about the left but that was all. Ban-the-bomb marches. None of this lunatic throw-the-bomb stuff then. Most of the kids went on the marches for the sex. Partly anyway.'

'So what about Miss Hibbert?'

'She's missing.'

'Oh.'

'She works for the American Embassy. She's been on leave. She hasn't reported back.'

52

'What are they going to do? Set the truant officer on her?'

'Please, Mrs Keatley.' Monk sounded almost embarrassed. 'This woman works close to their main security man. She could have known that Leskov had given your husband's name. She could have tipped him off.'

'What for? Old time's sake? In fond memory of a bit of heavy petting twenty-five years ago? Or is she another Kremlin super-spy?'

Molly was very angry and not sure why. Not jealousy, she hoped. Not after a quarter century and in these circumstances! No, she felt that Monk was in control of the exchange and that whatever she said was in response to some hidden cue. Her anger was generated by some form of ESP which was preparing her for worse to come.

'Mebbe,' said Monk. 'It was more than heavy petting, missus. She had his baby.'

'Oh no,' said Molly. This was a shock, but this was not it. There was more.

'Yes, missus. It died. But she had it and it was his. We found out when we were checking back on him. It didn't seem important, but every detail's noted. You never know. Then one of the Yanks mentioned this Hibbert woman being missing. She's not top grade security, but sensitive enough to be worth mentioning. Sally Ann Hibbert. The name rang a bell. We checked. It's the same one.'

'Tell me, Mr Monk, and don't be mealy-mouthed about it, are you trying to say that Sam and this woman have been seeing each other recently – having an affair, I mean?'

She had essayed a bell-like clarity of tone, but she stumbled at the end.

'No, missus,' said Monk. 'We know they've been seeing each other. Why, we don't know.'

'What? No two-way mirrors with hidden cameras? No blue films to show me?'

Monk sighed.

'No, missus. Perhaps he was. Perhaps he wasn't. Was it likely? You should know. It might have been a case of *once bitten twice shy* with this one. Your husband seems to have had a right scare with that business when he was a student.

53

That's likely why he had his operation soon as he could afford it.'

'Operation?' said Molly.

'You sound surprised, missus. Don't be. We're thorough, I tell you. We have to be. Medical history, political history, social history, emotional history, we do the lot. So you know nought of this Hibbert woman? Well, that fits, but I had to ask. Sorry to have troubled you. Here's a number to ring if anything does occur to you. The slightest thing. We're equipped to dea' with these matters, and you can't harm your husband now, missus.'

He thrust a card with a London telephone number on it into her hand.

'What operation?' said Molly, ESP at full blast.

'His vasectomy of course,' said Monk. 'Take care, missus.'

And he was gone, striding swiftly towards the leisure centre car park.

For a moment there was no anger, just sheer incredulous shock. Danny-boy pressed close against her legs as if in sympathy and she leaned heavily on his sturdy neck. But he sprang away as the rage came and she pushed herself upright, straightening like a longbow.

The bastard the bastard the fucking stinking bastard! she thought hysterically and did not know whether it was Sam or Monk she was thinking of. But she couldn't let him get away with this. He couldn't be allowed to drop seeds like these and walk off unchallenged. This had been his purpose, his sole nasty purpose. A woman. A baby. Sterility. Drop them, leave them, let them grow. See what they produced and whether it helped. Even her reaction now would probably be checked and counter-checked. Let it be! She had to know more.

'Mr Monk!' she called and was setting off in pursuit when she felt her arm grasped. Turning, she saw a tall stooping figure with his face shaded by the low-pulled brim of a Homburg and the high-folded collar of a belted raincoat. It was the Gestapo agent of the previous night, she was sure, and her anger against Monk was driven back by an onrush of terror. She tried to wrench free, but his grip was strong.

'Mrs Keatley, please. I have to talk with you.'

He had a high sing-song Welsh accent which set up a relieving sense of incongruity.

'It's not you I want to talk to, it's Monk,' she snarled, convinced that this was another security man.

'Please, Mrs Keatley. It's urgent. Your husband, where is he?'

'What?'

'I was hoping . . . had arranged . . . to see him. We're old . . . acquaintances. I don't know you but I've seen you . . . once. And the dog, of course, I know the dog. Please, Mrs Keatley, where is he?'

What was this? wondered Molly. Some crazy test? Provocation? Or just a delaying tactic?

'For all I know the bastard's washing dishes in the Kremlin!' she cried angrily. The grip relaxed as though she'd uttered a magic formula and she pushed the Welshman aside easily and ran into the car park with Danny gambolling around her, thoroughly enjoying the game.

Monk was nowhere to be seen, but her encounters were not finished.

A man was standing by the open boot of a car. In his hand he had a plastic grip from which protruded the shaft of a squash racket. He looked up at the sound of her hurrying feet, then came towards her. So programmed was she to seeking for Monk that she didn't recognize him until he spoke. It was Trevor Challenger.

'Molly, are you all right? Was that fellow bothering you?'

The Welshman must have taken a few tentative steps after her, but now, observing Trevor's intervention, he disappeared into the darkness of the field.

'Him? No. I was just looking for someone, that was all.'

'Who? If he's a member, I can probably tell you if he's around.'

The suggestion calmed her down more than anything else could have done.

'No, he's not a member,' she said, shaking her head. 'Come on, Danny-boy.'

'Why don't you come inside and have a drink? You'll probably know a lot of people. It's surprising how many of the old gang have taken it up.'

'What? Drinking?'

55

'Squash, I mean.'

'Well, it's safer than alcohol. No, thanks, Trev,' she said.

'Well, at least let me run you home in the car.'

'The exercise is the point of the exercise,' she said.

'You're very witty tonight,' said Trevor.

No, she thought. Angry. Confused. Post-Monkian depression. Would he lie to her about a thing like that? Would Sam not have told her? But if Monk was right, then there was so much Sam had not told her that a little thing like not being able to father children might easily have slipped his mind.

'Come on, Danny,' she said and headed back towards the field. The Welshman had seemed harmless and might be worth talking to now it seemed she had missed Monk.

Behind her she heard a car door slam viciously and thought with indifference that Trevor was still as childishly bad-tempered as ever. But a moment later he had overtaken her, minus his squash bag.

'You win,' he said.

'I'll be all right, Trevor,' she assured him.

'Oh, I know that,' he said. 'I'm here in case anyone attacks that poor dog.'

She laughed then and they walked in companionable silence for some time. She found that after all she was glad of the company.

'Penny for them,' he said.

'Old penny or new penny,' she said.

'Neither. I can guess. Working on the well-known principle that equal stimuli will produce equal reactions, I will merely tell you what I was thinking. I was remembering walking across here with you in the old days, before the leisure centre, or the new race-course grandstand, were built. I'd have been playing football and got changed and we'd be going back to your house for tea. And we'd hope like hell that when your dad went out to the Club, your mum would go with him. Am I right?'

No, thought Molly. I was wondering if I was Sam's dupe or Monk's dupe or the dupe of both of them. I was wondering if my husband had been deceiving me sexually as well as in all the other ways he seems to have been deceiving me. I was wondering if I would ever see him again, dead or alive.

I was wondering if I'd end my days in Doncaster or Moscow.

'Yes,' she said. 'More or less.'

'It must be fairly hectic being married to someone like Sam,' said Trevor, changing his tack. Molly was a little surprised. She had half anticipated a pursuit of the nostalgia theme leading up to an attempted embrace 'for old time's sake' before they reached the road.

'Fairly,' she said.

'Do you never go off to any of these exotic places with him?'

'He doesn't go all that often and the places aren't all that exotic and I'm not all that mad about being away from home anyway,' she said.

She tried to recollect if Sam had ever invited her along. No, he hadn't. If he was going to be spending his nights chatting up beautiful spies and mad scientists he'd hardly want her around. Or perhaps he just didn't want to risk involving her.

'A woman's place is in the home, eh?' said Trevor. 'You never used to think like that. First chance, goodbye Donny, off to London, bright lights. You know, I can hardly remember if you ever said goodbye!'

His tone was light, but she wasn't in the mood to be mature and worldly-wise and full of amused tolerance for the excesses of youth.

'Oh, we said goodbye, Trev,' she said coldly. 'I gave you the ring back. Did you manage to get a refund?'

'No,' he said quietly. 'I've still got it.'

Ah! Nostalgia fails. Regroup and try pathos.

'You should have had it re-set for Jennifer.'

'She didn't care for it,' said Trevor. 'By the way, she was wondering, that blond-haired chap you bumped into in the furniture department, it wasn't Jimmy Fardon's kid brother was it? You remember, used to live out at Balby.'

She mustn't underestimate this Trevor, she realized. Time didn't stand still, not even in Doncaster. He was no sitting target for the big city guns.

'No,' she said.

They were on the road now, but he gave no sign of turning back. She didn't mind. She was almost enjoying the company. As her mother had said that afternoon, it's best you've got something to occupy your mind.

'Jennifer looks well,' she said. 'What's the limit? You used to want a football team.'

'I'll settle for a tennis mixed doubles,' he said. 'What about you? Are you not going to bother?'

'No,' she said. 'Probably not.'

When they reached the house it was in darkness.

'Mum and Dad down the Club?' asked Trevor.

'I expect so.'

'Any chance of a cuppa?' he asked. 'It's a bit nippy without a top coat. I didn't expect to be walking.'

'It was your idea,' she said.

But she held the door open till he followed her into the house.

She watched with some amusement as he slipped into top gear. No wonder he hadn't tried his hand on Town Field. He had come a long way from lustful fumblings in the dark and chill open air. She recalled her mother's dark hints that the marriage was not without its troubles She had taken this to mean that Jennifer, a scion of the swarthy, half-gypsy Ramseys, had been free with her favours. But Trevor hadn't developed these well-oiled approaches by practising in front of the mirror.

She was all set to put him down with some well-judged gibe when the phone rang.

It was Monk. He was apologetic. It had occurred to him after they'd parted that he'd been less than diplomatic in telling her about the Hibbert woman. He had no intention of causing any distress, but he had a job to do. He hoped she would understand. He didn't mention the vasectomy.

Molly listened quietly. She felt surprisingly calm now. Rows on the telephone were no good to her. She assured him she was not in the least distressed. She was even about to mention the anxious Welshman when Monk said casually, 'Anyway, you're all right now?'

'Yes. I said.'

'I mean, this minute? Everything's all right at home?'

The bastard knows Trevor's here! she thought. And all her

fury came welling up again.

'Yes, I'm all right!' she said with heavy emphasis and slammed the receiver down.

She went back into the living-room. Trevor must have heard the violence with which she replaced the phone, or perhaps her emotion still showed on her face, for he looked anxiously at her and said, 'Everything all right?'

It was the last straw. She felt as if she must explode and somehow destroy for ever all these arrogant men who felt they could control her. Monk. Sam. Trevor.

'Yes, every bloody thing's all right!' she screamed.

He stepped back from her in surprise but she went after him and put herself provocatively close to him.

'For God's sake, Trev,' she said. 'Why don't you get on with it?'

Danny lay on the sofa and watched the activity on the mohair rug with great curiosity, working out how best to join in this new game.

When he was finished, Trevor pushed himself up on his hands and looked down at her with a kind of smug triumph.

'It's taken a long time,' he said.

'What?'

'This room. This rug. I'd given up any hope.'

'Ring Jennifer if you like and tell her you made it.'

His expression turned from man-of-the-world smug to little-boy hurt. Then Danny, thinking he'd worked out the rules, jumped on his back with a joyful howl.

'I'm glad he didn't do that earlier!' said Trevor as he got dressed.

Molly studied him carefully. It was unfortunate. Danny's intervention had caused them to share amusement and they were going to part friends. She was not sure if she wanted that.

At the door she prepared herself to rebuff any attempt to arrange another meeting. Instead he said casually, 'Everything *is* all right, is it, Molly?'

'Yes, of course, why shouldn't it be?'

'No reason. Except, well, any trouble, you know I'll help. OK?'

'OK,' she said.

She went back inside and tidied up all traces of activity in the living-room. It was quite late now, not too late to go down to the Club, but she didn't feel like it. Instead she watched television for a while, then took a pill and went to bed.

She was still awake when her mother opened the door and whispered her name. But she kept her eyes tightly closed and after a moment the door was pulled gently to and she heard her mother's footsteps going quietly down the stairs.

9

The telephone rang just as they were sitting down for their Sunday dinner. This was served at twelve-thirty sharp. Ivor Haddington might be lord of the night, but his wife ruled the lunch-hour with even more autocratic sway.

'Now who will that be?' said Mrs Haddington in tones full of the greatest irritation. 'Who'd ring at this time?'

Neither her husband, who was carving the rib of beef, nor Molly, who was pouring the wine she had contributed to the meal, ventured a guess, and Mrs Haddington went out of the room.

'Yes?' they heard her say. 'Who? Yes.'

She came back, irritation making way for disapproval.

'It's Trevor,' she said. 'For you.'

'For me?' said Molly.

'Yes. Don't be long at it else your dinner will be cold.'

Closing the door carefully behind her, Molly went into the hall and picked up the receiver.

'Molly?' said Trevor. She could hear a buzz of voices and the sound of music behind him.

'Hello, Trevor.'

'Hello. I haven't interrupted your meal, have I?'

'Just starting.'

'Oh, I'm sorry. I thought your mam sounded a bit off. I'd forgotten how early you ate on Sundays. It's been a long time.'

'It has,' agreed Molly. 'Is that what you wanted to tell me? And what's all that din?'

'I'm in the pub,' explained Trevor. 'I would have rung earlier but, well, it didn't seem worth taking the risk from home.'

'No, it wouldn't. Cheerio then, Trevor.'

'Hang on! I've not finished. I haven't really started. No,

61

it's just that after I'd left you last night, a funny thing happened. I went back to the leisure centre for my car. I had a quick drink when I was there, just a half . . .'

'For the alibi,' suggested Molly.

'If you like. Anyway, half way home I got stopped by the police and breathalyzed. I was quite all right, of course. But there were two of them and while one of them was sorting out the breathalyzer, the other one, a sergeant, went off with my licence and insurance papers. I was busy blowing into that damned bag, but I could see that the sergeant went up to his car and passed my papers through the window to someone in the back seat.'

'This is fascinating,' said Molly. 'I'd rather starve than miss any of this.'

'Wait a minute! He came back a minute later and handed them back to me. The test was negative, of course, so they waved me on. Well, I pulled out and as I passed their car, I had a quick glance inside. Now I know it was dark and the chap was sitting at the far side, but I'd put money on that it was the fellow you were talking to yesterday. The one with the bright blond hair.'

Behind Molly the living-room door opened.

'Molly!' called her mother. 'Your dinner will be ruined.'

'I'm coming, Mum,' she said. 'That's very interesting, Trevor. What am I supposed to do?'

'I don't know,' he said. 'I just thought I ought to tell you. Look, Sam couldn't be having you watched, could he? I mean, would he really have that kind of pull, getting the police in on the act?'

'Oh yes,' said Molly. 'He's got more pull than you could ever imagine, Trev. Thanks for ringing.'

She replaced the receiver before Trevor could say anything more. Her father's voice drifted out of the living-room.

'It's like newt piddle, this stuff.'

Thoughtfully she went back in.

'Sorry, Mum. Wine all right, Dad?'

'Grand,' he said.

'What did Trevor want?' asked her mother.

'He was having a drink with some of the old gang. Wondered if I'd like to pop along. I told him my dinner was on the table.'

'You want to watch that,' said Mrs Haddington significantly.

'I thought you liked Trev, Mum?'

'I like him well enough. But he's got a wife and kids and you've got a husband.'

'He's an old friend,' Molly protested.

'He's been a sight too friendly to a lot of people if half the stories are true. I just don't want him getting your name bandied about. So steer well clear of him, that's my advice.'

Molly regarded the mohair rug in front of the fireplace.

'Yes, Mum,' she said.

She contained her anger till later in the afternoon when she took Danny for a stroll. At the first telephone-box she came to, she dialled the operator, gave Monk's number, asking for person to person. 'And transfer the charges,' she added.

She got through quickly.

'Hello, missus,' came the now familiar flat voice.

'Listen,' said Molly in a low, furious tone. 'You keep off my friends, all right? Any more tricks like last night's and I'll start ringing the papers.'

To his credit, or discredit, he neither pretended ignorance nor offered justification.

'They won't print,' he said.

She was ready for this one.

'*Ici Paris* or *Stern.* They'll print.'

'Perhaps. It might not be big enough, missus,' he said, unruffled.

'I'll tell them that Princess Margaret's involved,' she said. 'I'm getting sick and tired of all this. I don't know where I am, I don't know what I'm doing, I don't even know what I *ought* to be doing. And having your lot snooping and prying all the time doesn't help a bit, not a bit. You understand me, Mr Monk?'

'Mr Challenger's an old friend?'

'Yes. Very old. I've known him since neither of us knew

Russia from Reigate. So leave him alone. Next time I see anyone hanging around, whether it's you or Aspinall or that
shifty Welshman, I'm going to start screaming. All right?'

'Hang on a sec, missus. What Welshman?'

'Oh, come on, Mr Monk!'

'You come on, missus. What Welshman?'

Sceptically, she told him about her encounter on Town
Field.

'You didn't say anything about this when I phoned you last
night,' he said accusingly.

'I wasn't in the mood for talking,' she said. 'Anyway, I
thought he was one of your creeps.'

'I need to know everything, Mrs Keatley. For your own
sake. And your husband's.'

He didn't sound convincing about Sam but she couldn't
tell him this as he'd rung off.

She walked slowly along the quiet Sunday streets with
Danny alternately towing and being towed. She hadn't been
lying when she told Monk that she didn't know what she ought
to be doing. Not that she wanted to hypocritically conform to
some acceptable norm, but it would be helpful if a norm existed
and she could see her own reactions in relation to it. Death
they talked about. Or divorce. Not that most people could
really prepare themselves, but at least they were talked about,
you saw people reacting to them, and there were certain ritual
frameworks, whether of law or religion, to structure the experience. This was different. This was worse than private, it
was a secret. She hadn't confided in a single soul – was that
normal? Even the Haddons had been brought in by Monk.
All she had done was run home to her mother. That sounded
a bit more normal. For a child.

And, of course, she had let an old boy-friend make love to
her in her parents' living-room. Before Sam, there had been
a couple of others, but no one else since. Unlike some of her
liberated friends, she had never felt able to contrast varying
techniques. Nor could she now. She could remember nothing
of either of them in action. The only pictures she could raise
were Sam running his fingers through his thick grey hair
and saying 'I'm sorry'; and Trevor all those years ago, his

features a pink blur through the mottled glass of the door she had just shut in his face.

Monday morning brought other worries. Selfishly Molly felt almost relieved.

Her mother's appointment with Dr Lamb was at nine-thirty. Molly waited till she heard her father go out to work, then came downstairs in her dressing-gown, a habit he disapproved of.

'Don't be long over your breakfast,' said Mrs Haddington. 'I want to be there on time.'

That meant at least fifteen minutes early. Normally Molly would have pointed out the foolishness of turning up before time, especially in a doctor's waiting-room, but this morning she said nothing. Instead she picked up the popular tabloid which brought the outside world to the Haddington household and flicked through the sheets.

DEFECTOR!

The word was headlined. Her vision blurred, her skin burnt, she felt sick. Seconds that felt like minutes passed before she could look again.

There was a picture beneath the huge letters. It wasn't Sam. But it was familiar. The last time she had seen that face, it had been creased with anxiety and shaded by a black homburg hat.

It was the Welshman who had spoken to her on Town Fields two nights previously. Quickly she went through the report. It seemed that Monk had been telling the truth. This was Dr Alan Llewellyn, member of a Ministry of Defence research unit attached to an RAF station in North Lincolnshire. It wasn't named. Either the paper didn't know or was paying lip-service to some Government directive.

Llewellyn had been interviewed in Oslo the previous day by a Norwegian journalist who had some slight acquaintance with him. Llewellyn was seeking political asylum in Russia, attracted by the greater scientific and personal freedom he felt awaited him there. But, with touching naïvety, he had obviously decided that his personal message of farewell to the country he was fleeing had a better chance of getting through unaltered if made while he was still on Western soil.

He was out of luck. Knowing something of the world of journalism, Molly could see what had happened. The Norwegian entrusted with this manifesto of truth and altruism had quickly worked out which British paper would pay best for the exclusive. And it wasn't the *Morning Star*. The message that came across was the self-justifying whine of a bitter, disappointed man. Perhaps it wasn't all that far from the truth. There was a lacerating leader full of contemptuous rhetoric.

Molly sat staring at the paper for a long time after she had finished the article. This was a foretaste of what lay in wait for Sam. The link between him and Llewellyn, whatever it was, could only make things worse.

'Molly, you haven't even started your breakfast! For heaven's sake, we can't keep Dr Lamb waiting!'

'He's bloody well kept you waiting,' she snapped angrily. Then, seeing the strain on her mother's face she was instantly contrite.

'I'm sorry, Mum. I'm not hungry. I'll just have my coffee, then I'll be straight with you.'

Dr Lamb had been the family doctor as long as Molly could remember. Presumably he had been young when she was a child, but she could not remember him as anything but old, and dried up. He saw them promptly, expressed great pleasure at seeing Molly again, made small talk about the changing face of Doncaster, and smiled a lot.

Molly knew the news was bad before he opened the file on his desk and let his little wizened face turn grave as though he were reading its contents for the first time.

'I'm afraid the tests have turned out to be positive, Mrs Haddington. It's no more than we feared, no more than we feared. Not that that's any comfort, of course, but it is no more, or less, than we feared.'

He nodded his head vigorously five times, then became very still, bright brown eyes staring unblinkingly into the space between mother and daughter.

Like a mummified marmoset, thought Molly.

'What exactly does that mean, doctor?' she enquired.

'It means, I'm afraid, treatment in hospital, a stay in hospital, I'm afraid,' said Lamb, returning to active life again.

'An operation?'

'Yes, I would think so, pretty certainly. No more than we expected.'

'A hysterectomy?'

'Yes, that's likely. Exploratory first, perhaps. Then a hysterectomy, pretty certainly.'

'When would this be, doctor?'

'I think the sooner the . . . no point in hanging about. I've been in touch. They can admit you this afternoon, Mrs Haddington. We've been very lucky. The operation would be, well, that would be up to the consultant. I'm glad you'll be at home, Molly. We don't want Mrs Haddington worrying about your father's meals, do we?'

Mrs Haddington had been sitting with that expression of blank interest she wore when waiting for a long-winded friend to pause for breath and let her in. Her left hand was clasped in Molly's right.

'Excuse me, Dr Lamb,' she said, leaning forward as though addressing someone deaf or a little stupid. 'What do you mean, positive?'

Someone had to say 'cancer', thought Molly. It was one of those few words which familiarity had rendered more instead of less potent. Her mother knew as well as she did what Dr Lamb was talking about. But the word had not been spoken. It was best to get it over with.

'Dr Lamb means the tests show that it's likely you've got cancer of the womb, Mum,' she said. 'You're to go into hospital to have an operation. He's fixed up for you to go in this afternoon.'

She should have let the doctor say it, she regretted instantly. Whoever spoke the word cast the spell.

Mrs Haddington's eyes turned towards her daughter and regarded her calmly as she let go of her hand.

'We'd best get something for Ivor's tea,' she said.

Back home, Molly phoned her father at his work. It took a long time to get him to understand what she was saying and by the time she put the phone down she was full of irritation. When he returned home the explaining and convincing had to be don: all over again but now instead of being irritated Molly was glad of it, as the circular question-and-answer narration going on between her parents assumed some of the cathartic qualities of ritual drama. Ivor's role was one of amazement that all this had gone on and he knew nothing of it. His wife in reply developed a kind of blasé superiority, shot through with moments of sheer exasperation at his stupidity. The perilous equilibrium was preserved till the moment of departure arrived. Mrs Haddington had declared that she was not going to have an ambulance coming to the door, that the hospital was close enough for her to walk, so Molly had summoned a taxi while the discussion was still in progress. But all conversation sputtered to silence when the taxi-driver rang the door bell. Ivor went ahead with the case, eager to be doing something. Mrs Haddington bustled round the living-room, doing a last minute tidy-up which even at this juncture filled Molly with her usual affectionate irritation. Then she was ready. One last glance which Molly only caught in the mirror above the mantelpiece. But it was a glance full of such pure despair that the moment seemed to freeze and there seemed to be no way of progressing beyond the naked absoluteness of that emotion.

Then Danny came bounding down the stairs to investigate the stir which had roused him from his afternoon nap in the bottom of the airing cupboard. He leapt up at Mrs Haddington, eager to charm her into a walk.

'Get away with you, you great stupid creature!' said Mrs Haddington. 'Molly, get him down! He'll catch my coat.'

And now she was ready for the neighbours.

At the hospital they sat and waited for over an hour until such time as Mrs Haddington's bed should be ready. Molly chatted brightly about this and that, trying to divert. Then changing her tack, she talked seriously but confidently about all the women she knew who'd had hysterectomies, stressing the ease and ordinariness of the operation.

'Yes, dear,' said Mrs Haddington, then turning to her husband she said, 'That nurse I spoke to when we came in, that's

Valerie Stringfellow's niece. I hope she's not on my ward. They're a terrible family for gossip.'

Molly got up and wandered off till she found a ward sister to complain to.

'We're terribly busy,' said the woman with a bright smile. 'It won't be much longer.'

'If you're so busy why don't you suggest reasonable times for people to turn up at?' demanded Molly. 'My mother would be better off sitting in her own home till you were ready for her.'

'I'm afraid we don't decide times of admission,' said the sister.

'What *do* you do then? Good God, it's only a *bed* to make, isn't it? I mean, you've *got* the bed? You're not having to send out to buy it or something, are you?'

Molly was amazed at what the crises in her life were doing to her. Only a couple of weeks ago the thought of having to tell a waiter that he'd brought the soup when she'd ordered the melon would have caused an agony of embarrassment. Now she could hardly open her mouth without having a go at someone. It was as if she too had been a spy, acting out a role of placid amiability to fool the establishment. Perhaps if she met Sam again the new *she* and the new *he* would fall in love and be able to find a new, vital, active excitement to replace the old easygoing contentment she had thought they shared.

When she got back to the waiting area she found her mother being led to the ward by Valerie Stringfellow's niece.

'And how's your Uncle Joe?' Mrs Haddington was saying. 'Does he still have the pigeons? Thank heaven that's one thing that Ivor never hankered after. We've got a dog, and he's bad enough, but them things on your roof!'

'Shall I come in and give you a hand, Mum?' said Molly.

'Certainly not,' said Mrs Haddington. 'I can get into bed myself. I'm not that decrepit.'

'Give her ten minutes, then come on in,' suggested the nurse. 'Come along, Mrs Haddington.'

Appetite is the last victim of a Yorkshireman's strong emotion and Mr Haddington cleared his plate that evening as thoroughly as ever, but with a mechanical series of movements that hinted a total indifference to what was going into his mouth.

'Did you enjoy those chops, Dad?' enquired Molly as he chewed the last piece of gammon.

'Grand,' he said. 'Will they feed your mother?'

'No, they'll let her starve!' said Molly, laughing. Ivor hated hospitals so much that he had managed to shut out of his mind all knowledge of their organization and method.

'She'll be all right?' he said. 'Won't she?'

'Of course she'll be all right,' said Molly.

'All this happening and I knew nowt. Tight-lipped. She talks the hind-leg off a donkey, yet she'll tell you nowt she doesn't want you to know. It's not good, hiding things. Not in families.'

'No,' said Molly. 'I think you're right.'

At visiting time that night, they discovered that the doctor had said hello to Mrs Haddington on his evening rounds but nothing more.

'Hasn't she been examined?' Molly asked the ward sister.

'Tomorrow. She'll be examined tomorrow.'

'What is she doing in here tonight then?'

'We like them to have a bit of time to settle. It's for the best, really it is.'

'Jesus,' said Molly. 'She only lives half a mile away. Settling in! If I took her home now, what time would you want her back in the morning?'

'She's really settling in very nicely. It would be a shame to upset her,' said the sister.

And she was right, of course. Mrs Haddington was in a four bed sub-ward and she had already set about establishing a moral dominance over the three other inmates. Molly returning from the sister's office heard her mother's voice while she was still in the corridor.

'. . . married to Sam Keatley. He's a journalist, he's sometimes on the television. Current affairs, those science programmes where they talk. *You* might not watch them. I watch a lot of them. I don't care for plays and quizzes and such. He's abroad at the moment. Molly, love, I was just telling this lady here, which country is it that Sam's in just now?'

'This lady here', a frail old woman, with one even frailer-looking visitor, presumably her husband, smiled vaguely in Molly's direction from the next bed.

Molly managed to smile back. Complementary to her mother's reticence in matters which she judged were her own business was her enthusiasm for broadcasting anything she felt redounded to the family's credit. The lack of grandchildren had always been felt as a grave disadvantage in the battle for local supremacy, but Sam's job was worked for all it was worth.

Which, she thought cynically, was a damn sight less than her mother imagined.

She hoped to God the news didn't break while her mother was in hospital. The local papers would sniff out the connection soon enough.

But, in or out of hospital, Mrs Haddington would find plenty of people ready to recall her flourishing of Sam's profession as a trump card in the happy-and-successful-families game.

'Poland,' she said at random. 'Sam's in Poland.'

'Oh,' said her mother. 'I thought you said he was going to Austria when you rang.'

Molly couldn't remember what she'd said.

'He moves around a lot,' she said.

Mrs Haddington smiled benevolently at the old lady and everyone else in the room.

'He moves around a lot,' she said.

The phone rang at two a.m. Molly who had been lying wide awake went shivering down the stairs and took the call.

The line was full of noises; clicks and skirls as of distant bagpipes. Then came a woman's voice, also distant, saying something with a questioning intonation in a language Molly didn't recognize. Finally a man's voice said very clearly 'Hello!' and after that the line went dead.

Molly smoked a cigarette in the kitchen. When she went back to bed she fell asleep almost immediately.

IO

'Happen I should take a few days off work,' said Ivor Haddington at breakfast.

Molly drank her coffee and looked over the rim of the mug. He was asking for her advice, she realized.

'Happen,' she said. 'But not yet awhile, Dad. You know what Mum's like. She'll get really worried if she thought you were hanging around here all day.'

'You'd leave it, then?'

'Till we see how things go. They'll be looking at her this morning. I'll go up in the afternoon and see what's what. And we can both go tonight.'

'Right,' he said. 'I'll be off.'

He got up and went out, returning a moment later wearing his flat cloth cap, set perfectly straight on his head, and his leather-bound donkey-jacket. He reached up behind the kitchen door to where his old ex-army knapsack hung limply. As he felt its emptiness his face changed, and the strong worn leather of his skin sagged flaccidly like the webbing in his hand. Molly in her mind's eye saw her mother every morning filling the flask with tea and the snap-box with sandwiches, packing them into the knapsack and hanging them ready behind the door.

'Oh Dad,' she said. 'I'm sorry. I forgot.'

'No matter,' he said, turning his back on her and carefully replacing the knapsack on the hook. 'I'll brew up at work.'

'I am sorry,' said Molly. Not for forgetting, but for reminding. Routine is selfish. Not once in forty years would Ivor have thanked his wife for her care in the preparation of his food. But such familiar neglect quietly stores up its proper pain. Molly had found this out.

'I'm off then,' said Ivor. 'Back for tea.'

72

Now even the formula used every day of his working life would sound strangely on his newly sensitive ears.

For Christ's sake! thought Molly. I'm thinking as if Mum's dead!

She set about clearing up, then decided to give the whole house a good clean. But first Danny had to be taken for a walk. And when she got back, she found her cleaning plans had to be postponed. Someone, perhaps Valerie Stringfellow's niece, had done a good job of passing the word and during the course of the morning there were five anxious visitors and as many telephone calls. At last about midday Molly shut the door on the last of the callers and flopped into a chair, clutching a glass of her father's whisky. She had just set it to her lips when the doorbell rang again.

'Oh no,' she said.

She would have ignored it except that Danny was running in and out of the living-room barking loudly to tell her there was someone at the door. Everyone familiar with the household knew that Danny only barked if there was someone at home. It was a standing joke that you could break in when Danny was by himself and he wouldn't utter a sound.

Hoping that it was someone who could be dealt with on the doorstep, Molly opened the door.

It was Monk. At least she wouldn't need to repeat the formulas of her mother's hospitalization, she thought. On the other hand, he wasn't going to be dealt with on the doorstep.

'Come in,' she said.

'Thanks, missus,' he said, stepping inside and wiping his feet with the exaggerated vigour of a working-class housetraining.

'I'm sorry to hear about your mother,' he said.

'Not you too!' exclaimed Molly. 'How did you hear? No, sorry. I'm being silly. Knowing how you lot work, you probably heard it before I did!'

'Someone mentioned hospitals,' said Monk. 'We checked. In case it was you.'

'Slashing my wrists, you mean?'

'I couldn't see it myself,' said Monk. 'Cancer, is it? It'll be all right if it hasn't got too far.'

'You'll keep an eye on it, will you?' said Molly. 'See it doesn't leave the country?'

Monk ignored her. He had taken off his soiled riding mac to reveal the crumpled blue suit. Molly noticed that the same two buttons of his cardigan were undone. Perhaps he never undressed. More likely, he just pulled it on and off over his head.

'You knew nothing of this before you came?' enquired Monk.

'About Mum? No. None of us did.'

'But you were *planning* to come up this weekend, were you?'

Molly looked at him in surprise.

'Of course. I talked about it with you.'

'I mean, you and your husband? If all this hadn't happened. You had *planned* to come up on a visit?'

'Yes,' said Molly. 'Just for the weekend, of course. My mother rang to remind me and I said I'd be coming by myself because Sam had to go away. I'm sure I told you.'

'No, missus. Not that you would both have been visiting here this weekend.'

'What difference does it make?' demanded Molly. 'You're damned lucky I tell you anything!'

'You don't tell us much, missus,' said Monk grimly. 'You didn't let on about meeting Dr Llewellyn, did you?'

'I didn't know who he was!' protested Molly. 'And I mentioned him next day.'

Suddenly thoughts began to run together in her mind. She took a long sip at her whisky.

'You're not suggesting that when Sam came up here, he . . .'

She tailed off. Why sound ridiculous in front of Monk? If Sam was working for the Russians, why the hell should he stop just because he'd come to Yorkshire? But she recalled how willingly he'd always agreed to join her on her visits home, how pleased he'd always seemed to be at meeting her parents. And, despite his pretended horror at dogs, how keen he'd been to take Danny out for his evening walks. *We're best by ourselves, he'd say. We understand each other. I won't crap on him if he doesn't crap on me.*

'Yes, missus,' said Monk. 'You don't think Llewellyn was hanging around Town Fields hoping for a pick-up, do you?'

'What do you mean?' said Molly hopelessly.

'We reckon he had a date with your husband. They'd probably met up here a few times before. It was too good a chance to miss, your parents living in Doncaster, Llewellyn's research group working just a few miles to the south. Your man had to get out too quickly to send any warnings. Llewellyn expected to see him on Friday night. Instead he saw you.'

'He wouldn't know me.'

'He'd know that thing,' said Monk, looking towards Danny who was lying on the rug observing Monk with every sign of great adoration.

'He didn't seem like a spy,' said Molly, aware once more that she was saying something absurd. But Monk did not take it so.

'No. You're right, missus. Llewellyn's no spy. Just a run-of-the-mill scientist without a proper conceit of himself. He doesn't sell secrets. He gives them away so he can feel important. It's called idealism. Funny thing is, he didn't really know enough to make us rate him very high!'

'You suspected him though?'

Monk shrugged.

'What's suspected? He was on a grey list, one of a dozen or more who could have passed on a certain item we knew the Russians got a few months past. Nothing important. If he'd kept still we'd not have noticed him. Or if you'd told us right away, we might have got him.'

'Wasn't he being watched?'

'What do you think we are, missus?' said Monk bitterly. 'An army? I've got ten men and they're worked so hard, there's usually a couple off sick.'

'You were watching me that night,' she protested with equal bitterness.

'I told young Aspinall to see you safe home,' he said. 'It's no place for a young woman to be patrolling alone. This thing here would likely stand by wagging its tail if you got attacked.'

Danny nodded his huge head vigorously as though in agreement. Molly didn't know whether to laugh or be touched. What was peculiar was that she had no difficulty in believing Monk's concern.

Monk continued.

'Then he sees you meet this other fellow in the car park soon as I'm gone and you take him home with you. It had to be checked.'

'If he'd been a bit sharper, he'd have seen Llewellyn,' retorted Molly.

'My fault,' said Monk. 'I kept him talking. Even then, if you'd told me on the phone. Llewellyn went straight off, drove to Hull, got on a boat. There's any amount now. They come across in droves for the bargains in Marks' and Tesco's. He wasn't missed. He's not married, lives alone, wasn't due anywhere till Monday. By the time we began to check, he was making that pathetic speech in Oslo. Then straight on a plane heading East. Poor sod.'

'What'll happen to him?' asked Molly.

'He'll have a bit of propaganda value. Then they'll work him a bit. Nothing exciting, he's not that good. And nothing important. What can bend one way can be bent back. Once the honeymoon's over, he'll be worse off than here. Less status, less money, less freedom, less hope. He'll jump off a bridge some night, or get pushed. Depends whether he lets it eat away inside him or starts griping.'

Molly finished her drink and rose to pour herself another. She gestured with the bottle towards Monk, who shook his head.

'Are we talking about Sam too, Mr Monk?' she asked in a clear high voice.

Monk shook his head again.

'No, missus. If it's any consolation to you, we're not. Llewellyn's a bit pathetic. Your husband's not that. He's been a real boon to them and he's done this country real harm. They honour their own. And he'll be of some real use to them in their training schools.'

'Training?'

'Agents. Media manipulation. That stuff. He'll do all right.'

'You never said any of this to me before,' said Molly thoughtfully.

'I thought it better to play up the squalid little traitor angle, missus. You said you couldn't believe that. Do you find the Hero of the Soviet Union any easier to believe in?'

Molly took a deep breath and spoke in her best mature self-contained voice.

'As I imagine you know, Mr Monk, I'm finding it very hard to believe in anything at all just now. Except my mother being in hospital, and I'd prefer not to believe in that. But it's a fact. I'll have to go there shortly to see what they plan to do to her, how much they plan to cut open, and to cut out, and when, and why, and which, and what, and who . . .'

She was still standing and found herself swaying slightly in time to the rhythms of her phrasing. She wanted to remain cool and self-possessed in front of Monk, but if she couldn't quite manage this, a rhythmic chant seemed preferable to a tearful incoherence.

Monk took the glass from her hands, set it down on the table and put his arm awkwardly around her shoulders to lead her to a chair. He smelt of soap, which surprised her. She must have subconsciously decided that at close quarters those awful old clothes would be distinctly musty. Instead, all she could smell was plain unperfumed soap. It was such a homely, honest smell that her hysteria died away as if put to shame.

'You'd better have something to eat,' he said. 'We don't want you in hospital too, missus.'

Whether this was an expression of general concern for her well-being or a hint of some other as yet secret and therefore sinister fate awaiting her, she could not decide. He heated up a tin of Irish Stew which he set before her accompanied by two grossly thick slices of bread.

'I don't like Irish Stew,' she said.

She ate it all and wiped the plate with the bread before devouring that too.

'I meant I never used to like Irish Stew,' she said. 'When I was a girl, in this house, I would never eat it. It was, still is, one of Dad's favourites. I'd sit here, at this very table, stead-fastly refusing to take a mouthful. They'd say I couldn't get

77

down till it was all gone. Then there'd be compromises. I could leave the carrots. The onions. All I had to do was pick out the meat. Finally it'd end up with a single spoonful. If I ate one spoonful, I could get down. Then I'd take a very little spoonful and put it in my mouth and quietly leave the table and go up to the lavatory and spit it out. Tell me, Mr Monk. All that you told me about Sam and that American girl, and having the vasectomy, was that true? Or was it just part of your make-me-think-he's-a-rat campaign?'

'True, missus. I'm sorry.'

'Then I don't know him, do I? Won't you have something to eat, Mr Monk?'

'No, thanks. But I'll have that drink.'

'Now I've stopped? Help yourself. I'll make a coffee. No, really. I'm fine. Coffee and a bit of fruit cake, then I'll be ready for anything.'

She went into the kitchen and put the kettle on. While it was boiling she cut herself a piece of her mother's fruit cake, using the small carving knife which Ivor kept honed like a razor. The ease with which it sliced through the heavy cake troubled her and she washed and dried it very carefully and put it away before making the coffee.

'Why're you still bothering with me, Mr Monk?' she asked as she returned to the living-room. 'Do you still suspect I'm in this with Sam?'

He shook his head.

'Why then?'

'You're our main point of contact, missus.'

'Am I? With *what*?' she asked mockingly.

'Llewellyn got in touch, didn't he?'

'What's that mean? You're going to set me and Danny walking round public parks up and down the country in the hope that foreign agents are going to go *psst!* from the bushes?'

'If I thought it'd do any good, I'd do it,' said Monk seriously. 'No, missus. But until your man surfaces, we've got to assume he can be anywhere.'

Molly spluttered through her fruit cake.

'You mean, you think he could just have taken cover in England and be ready to pop up to see me any time?'

'It's a chance we can't ignore,' said Monk.

'Oh yes you can,' said Molly. 'Forget it. He's abroad all right. He tried to ring me last night. And it wasn't from Brighton.'

Monk took her up to the hospital in a Ford Escort which sounded as though it could do with medical treatment. Monk had seemed unimpressed by her news about the phone call. Perhaps the line was tapped and he knew about it already. Or perhaps he was simply not prepared to accept an insomniac woman's identification of her husband's voice on the strength of a single word.

'Will you go back to London now?' she asked as she got out of the car.

'Mebbe. We're just checking Llewellyn out. In case he's left a friend.'

'It's not enough to be corrupt yourself. You must also corrupt a friend,' said Molly in a quoting voice.

'Did someone say that, missus?'

'Someone should have. I suppose you'll be in touch, Mr Monk.'

'I'd prefer you got in touch with me,' he said. 'If your husband's abroad, he's safe. You can't harm him. So just let me know if there's anything else happens. Any little thing.'

'Just a spoonful, Mr Monk? Just a little spoonful? And no onions!'

'I hope your mother's all right, missus. Take care.'

To her surprise he reached out and took her hand and gave it a hard squeeze. Then he drove away. He was not a fast or a flashy driver but he progressed with a steady inexorability which made other drivers give way.

Molly went into the hospital to find the screens round her mother's bed.

'She's been ever so upset,' whispered the frail old lady who was eating boiled sweets and reading Jean Plaidy. 'I tried to help but I could see it were no use. They've given her a tranquillizer.'

Molly felt sick with fear but when she got behind the screen she found her mother holding a compact mirror and peering at her face through a cloud of powder.

'Mum! What are you doing?' she asked.

'Making myself presentable,' said Mrs Haddington. 'Pull them screens back, will you? They'll be thinking I'm dead.'

'I thought they'd given you something.'

'They did,' said Mrs Haddington. 'Two pills. But I only swallowed the one. There now. Go on. Make yourself useful. Move them things.'

She put a final cloudy dab on her cheek and obediently Molly began to fold back the screen.

'What are you doing?' asked a nurse who had just come into the room.

'I'm moving this screen.'

The nurse regarded her uncertainly, then went out and returned almost immediately with the ward sister.

'It's Mrs Haddington's daughter, is it? Could I have a word?' she said.

'Back in a moment, Mum,' said Molly.

'I wanted to see you before you went in,' said the sister neutrally.

'Then you should have been around,' said Molly politely.

'The thing is, your mother was examined this morning and she had a talk with the doctor. She seemed to be in good control so he saw no reason not to tell her the truth.'

'I'm glad he didn't see any reason to lie,' said Molly.

'I'm afraid they will have to operate,' said the sister more abruptly than perhaps she had intended.

'Yes?' said Molly. 'Is that it?'

'Oh,' said the sister. 'I wish your mother could have taken it so well.'

'I'd have been more inclined to hysterics if you'd told me they were going to try embrocation and a bit of massage,' said Molly. 'What did my mother say?'

'She got herself very upset. We were surprised. She'd seemed so well balanced.'

'I think the balance is back,' said Molly. 'I'll go and ask her.'

The sister reached out a hand and grasped at Molly's sleeve.

'I really think . . . she's been tranquillized . . . a little rest, then come back tonight, please.'

'I'll stay a while,' said Molly, disengaging herself. 'When is the operation taking place?'

'Mr Sterling was hoping to fit her in at the end of the week. Friday.'

'Hoping?' said Molly.

'You know how these things are,' said the sister. 'Mr Sterling has a very crowded schedule. It just needs something, an emergency . . .'

'I'll tell you what,' said Molly gently. 'If you or anybody get my mother ready for an operation on Friday, and for any reason she doesn't have it, then you'll really know what an emergency's all about. I'd like to speak to Mr Sterling if I may.'

After some demur, the sister made a telephone call and with an ease which clearly embarrassed her arranged an appointment for two p.m. the following day.

Molly went back into the ward to find Mrs Haddington telling the frail old lady why she would find the ending of her Jean Plaidy novel unsatisfactory. Molly sat by the bed and took her mother's hand. For her pains she received a sympathetic squeeze and a comforting smile. She didn't mind. She was finding out herself that control, unlike charity, begins away from home. And Monk's farewell gesture had reminded her of the simple comfort to be got from holding hands.

II

When she arrived home, a man got out of a blue Cortina parked opposite the house and followed her up the path.

'Mrs Keatley?' he said.

She ignored him, turned the key in the door and opened it so that Danny, silent in the empty house, could see her and start his welcoming bark which was certainly worse than any bite that gentlest of mouths was ever likely to inflict.

Now she turned.

'Yes?'

The man was about thirty, black-haired, thin-faced, with a bulbous nose that didn't quite match, wearing a smart blue velvet jacket over a grey roll-neck sweater.

'Could I have a word, Mrs Keatley? It's about your husband. Sam.'

'You're a friend of my husband's?' she asked, alert to the nuance of the Christian name.

'In a way,' he said. 'We haven't met recently, though. If you could spare just a moment.'

For a second she'd thought he was another of Monk's men, or (more far-fetched) some courier from behind the Iron Curtain. But now she had him placed. He was a journalist. She kept the knowledge from her face.

'I'm afraid Sam's not here,' she said. 'I'm just by myself, Mr . . . ?'

'Wallace.' he said. 'That's really where I hoped you could help me, Mrs Keatley. Do you know where your husband is?'

'Not precisely,' said Molly. 'Won't you step inside? He's a journalist; well, you'd know that if you know him. And he travels around quite a bit. He's on the Continent at the moment.'

'I see,' said Wallace, following her into the living-room

with many an uneasy look at Danny-boy. 'Have you heard from him recently?'

'Not recently,' said Molly. 'I'll tell you what, Mr Wallace, I can soon find out where he is, if you care to hang on a minute. Danny will keep you company, won't you, boy?'

She retreated into the hall and picked up the phone. Her first impulse was to phone Monk's number, but now she hesitated. He certainly wouldn't be back in London yet and by the time they got on to him the emergency, if emergency it were, would have passed. In addition, another idea had started up in her mind.

She dialled the number of *The New Technocrat* and asked for Iain Haddon.

'Iain,' she said. 'This is Molly Keatley.'

'Hello, Molly,' he said. 'How are you? We've all been thinking about you.'

'I thought you must have been,' she said. 'I've got a man called Wallace here. He says you sent him.'

Through the open living-room door she saw Wallace's face grow even more perturbed than Danny's attempts to lick it off could account for.

There was a silence at the other end of the line which stretched out beyond puzzlement into guilt.

'Oh shit,' said Haddon finally.

'Yes, Iain?'

'I'm sorry, Molly,' he said. 'I owed him a favour. But it was just the address I gave him, believe me. He was hot on the scent already. He's been doing a feature on Leskov for the *Telegraph*. Leskov's the Russian who – '

'Yes, I know.'

'Evidently something he picked up via Leskov put Wallace on Sam's track. He came round to see me. Naturally I couldn't, wouldn't, tell him anything; but your address, there seemed no harm. He'd have found it somehow. But I'm sorry, Molly. Anyway, what's the news? Have you heard anything more about Sam?'

'Not really,' said Molly. 'But don't worry, Iain, I remember favours too. As soon as anything breaks, I'll see you're one of the first to get the newspaper. 'Bye.'

She went back into the living-room.

'Danny, get down,' she said. 'Be careful what you lick.'

'That was hardly fair, Mrs Keatley,' the man said.

'You said you were a friend of my husband's,' she replied. 'And Iain Haddon. He *was* a friend.'

'Haddon only gave me this address,' said Wallace. 'And I *did* know your husband. Only vaguely, true. But the way things have turned out, that's the way everybody knew him. Me. Haddon. And what about you, Mrs Keatley?'

'What?'

'Did you know him any better? Were you completely surprised by all this?'

'All what?'

Wallace smiled, a broad clown's smile. The bulb-like nose should have lit up too, thought Molly.

'No, I'm not setting a cunning gutter-press trap,' he said. 'Here's what I think happened. Leskov gave Sam's name to the CIA who passed it on to British Security. Sam got wind of it and took off. Now everyone's hanging around waiting for the opposition to make things public. No one's going to print anything till then – I mean, it can cost a paper a lot of money if it says someone's defected, then he turns up from having a dirty weekend in Paris. All I want is to be first with the inside story when it all breaks. Is that bad?'

Molly looked at him and wondered how a journalist could get on to such a well-screened story as this. So much for Monk's security!

'It doesn't strike me as being particularly good,' she said.

'Sam'll get as good a press as you can hope for from me,' he said. 'Science is universal, a secret shared is a danger halved, hands across the tundra, all that sort of thing. There'll be others who'll want to hang, draw and quarter him, but at least I'd have got in first.'

Molly sat down and leaned heavily on Danny to stop him from trying to jump on to her lap.

'Perhaps I'd *like* him to be hung, drawn and quartered,' she said.

'I take it that means you knew nothing about his activities till he went,' said Wallace.

Molly smiled sweetly at him.

'The only thing you can take is your leave, Mr Wallace,'

she said. 'I've no idea what you've been talking about and therefore I am quite unable to comment.'

To her surprise he seemed prepared to accept his dismissal with a good grace.

'I'll be in touch,' he said as he stood on the doorstep.

'It's your time,' she answered.

He looked at her speculatively and she felt that he was debating whether to tell her something important. But in the end he decided against it. For now.

'You're on an island, Mrs Keatley,' he said. 'But you can't stay there. And don't imagine you're alone.'

'I'm not,' she said. 'But I will be. Goodbye, Mr Wallace.'

She sat on the stairs and talked to Danny after closing the door.

'What's to be done, you great lump?' she asked. 'He's right, isn't he? I am on an island, and a precious little one it is. Much more crowding and I'm going to be pushed off. There's a white sea raging down there, Dan. It doesn't look much from above. Quite flat and calm really. But it's raging all right, believe me, and I'm frightened of tumbling into it. So what shall I do?'

She pulled Danny's ears, and he barked excitedly and ran back and forwards between her and the door.

'Go for a walk?' she said, smiling. 'That's your answer to everything. But you can't walk far on a crowded cliff.'

She went to the telephone and dialled Monk's London number.

'Yes?' said a neutral voice. It sounded like the ward sister.

'This is Molly Keatley. Tell Mr Monk a journalist called Wallace has been to see me. Iain Haddon at *The New Technocrat* gave him my address. Wallace seems to know everything.'

She put the receiver down without waiting for an acknowledgement.

'All right,' she said to Danny. 'Now we'll try it your way.'

It started raining while she was out with Danny and by the time her father got home it was pouring down.

'Get out of those things quick, Dad,' she said, 'or we'll

85

be having you in hospital too.'

'You sound just like your mam,' said Ivor. 'What's the news?'

He stood dripping on to the kitchen floor while she told him, then went and got changed without any comment.

When he returned to the kitchen, Molly was pushing sausages around the frying-pan, and keeping a watchful eye on a panful of chips.

'Friday,' said Ivor. 'And it's Tuesday today.'

'And tomorrow will be Wednesday,' said Molly.

'That's a poser,' said Ivor. 'They have to do it? There's no other way?'

'I'm afraid not,' said Molly. 'It'll be all right, Dad. You'll see.'

'Mebbe so. Will we be able to see her before, like?'

'Of course we will. They don't lock them up, you know. Seven-thirty till eight-thirty tonight.'

'I hope the rain stops,' said Ivor.

The phone rang.

'Will you see to that, Dad?' said Molly. 'These chips are about done.'

She heard his voice in the hall. His telephone conversations were always conducted in monosyllables and it was impossible to work out what was going on.

She had drained the chips and was putting the food on to plates when he returned.

'That was Trevor's missus, Jennifer,' he said.

'Jennifer Challenger?' said Molly, surprised. 'What did she want?'

'She'd heard about your mam. Wanted to know if it was true. She said she were sorry.'

'That was nice of her,' said Molly. 'Do you want HP *and* tomato sauce?'

'She's sending Trev to take us to the hospital.'

'She's what?'

'Aye. She asked how we were getting there tonight. I said likely we'd walk, it's no distance really, but she said we'd get soaked. So she's sending Trev to pick us up.'

'There's no need!' protested Molly. 'If the weather's that bad, I'd ring for a taxi.'

'You've saved your brass then, haven't you?' said Ivor.

Bitch, thought Molly. Lending me her husband. If it's interest she's after, she might get more than she's bargained for.

'Have you let Sam know?' asked her father.

'What?'

'About your mam. He'd want to know. He thinks a lot of your mam.'

'Yes, he does.'

Or does he? How did she know what or who it was that Sam really thought a lot of? At least her mother was one of the exploited proletariat (though she'd have thumped anyone who told her so) and affection for her would fit the party line better than his apparent fondness for members of the high bourgeoisie like the Haddons.

'No,' she said. 'I haven't been able to get in touch. It's difficult at the moment.'

'He'd want to know,' repeated her father.

The rain had almost stopped by the time Trevor called for them, but she was glad of the lift if only because she had found herself running out of bright shafts of optimism to cast into the dark clouds which had settled over her father. Seated alone in the back seat she was able to close her eyes and let the movement of the car soothe her like a cradle while Trevor spoke seriously to her father of his hopes for an early improvement in Doncaster Rovers' fortunes.

In the ward, Molly saw with relief that the screen had not been re-erected round her mother's bed. Mrs Haddington was now totally recovered both from her depression and her sedation and had clearly been using the imminence of her operation to confirm her ascendancy over the other patients. When she saw Trevor she shot a glance, simultaneously enquiring and accusing, at Molly, but the large bouquet of flowers he produced tipped the scales in his favour. Ivor she subjected to a close cross-questioning to establish that his needs were being properly taken care of in her absence. The ward sister put in a brief appearance to point out that two visitors at a time was the rule, but Trevor turned on the charm and even made the woman laugh before she went off, placated. Her own reaction had been to ask the sister what she intended to do about it. But Trevor's response did just as well. Only Ivor's look of guilt and instinctive movement out of his chair annoyed her.

After half an hour Trevor rose and said he'd wait outside.

'No need,' said Mrs Haddington.

'You'll want a bit of time alone with your family,' said Trevor.

Leaning over the bed he kissed her forehead and said, 'See you again soon. Take care.'

'Nice lad,' said Mrs Haddington as she watched him go.

'That's probably what all his girl-friends say,' observed Molly.

Ten minutes from the end of visiting time she rose too.

'I'll let you and Dad have a moment,' she said. Ivor looked up at her as though she'd pulled his chair from under him. 'See you tomorrow, Mum.'

'Don't forget to bring that knitting,' said her mother. 'I might as well do something useful while I'm stuck in here.'

Trevor was leaning on the reception counter chatting earnestly to the sister and another nurse.

'Hello,' he said. 'Time up already?'

'Not quite. I left Dad to have a private chat.'

'Very diplomatic. See you, ladies.'

He accompanied her to the tiny waiting-room.

'She seems in good spirits,' he said.

'Yes. You too.'

'Sorry?'

'I see that all those rumours I've heard about you are true.'

'What rumours?'

'The Don Juan of Donnie.'

He looked so pleased with himself that she went on, 'I was surprised. You used to be so gowkish.'

'Did I?'

'Oh yes. I think that's why I gave you up. No one else was interested in you. I couldn't marry a man who didn't make me jealous.'

'Well, you were wrong, weren't you? I was soon snapped up.'

'Snapped? I'd say gobbled.'

'That's not very nice,' he said. 'Still, perhaps it was for the best. If I'd married you, I might have stayed faithful. And gowkish.'

'I've suddenly realized why goats are symbols of lechery,' she said. 'It's not because of their performance, but because they eat up everything you give them. There's nothing they'll choke on.'

'Why do you want to make me choke?' he asked. 'Because of the other night?'

'That?' she said, smiling. 'Of course not. After all, that was my choice.'

'Yes, it was,' he said thoughtfully. 'I wondered about that. Then that other business with the police afterwards. Is something wrong between you and Sam? Are you in some kind of trouble?'

'No trouble,' she said. 'The situation is hopeless but not desperate.'

'You've changed too,' he said. 'You used to be . . . springy.'

'Vernal?' she said. 'Or like a trampoline?'

'That's what I mean,' he said. 'You used to be not like this. But I'm not complaining. Are we going to see each other again?'

'If Jennifer puts you on transport detail again, I suppose so.'

'You know what I mean,' he said. 'You owe me something.'

She was genuinely astounded.

'What? You've got a wife. Two kids. Another on the way. A good job. Even a house in Sprotbrough.'

'It's still Doncaster,' he said. 'With you I think I'd have got away.'

'With me . . .! Well, Trev, you shouldn't have been so gowkish!'

She suddenly laughed and added, 'At that rate, you'd never guess how much *you* owe *me*!'

The door opened and Ivor's head appeared.

'Chucking-out time,' he said with evident relief.

On the way home he asked rather shame-facedly if Trevor would mind dropping him at the Club.

'He's worried about how he should behave,' said Molly as they drove away from the forlorn-looking figure on the pavement. 'He thinks he shouldn't want to have his pint and see his mates.'

'It hasn't stopped him, has it?' said Trevor.

'Life's a downhill run,' said Molly. 'Hard to stop.'

When they reached Rothwell Avenue, Trevor stopped the car a good distance from the house and looked at Molly enquiringly.

'No,' she said. 'Jennifer knows what visiting hours are and she'll be timing you home.'

'Is that the only reason?'

She leaned over and kissed him lightly but full on the lips.

'It's good enough,' she said as she got out of the car.

'Molly,' he said through the open window. '*Is* there something wrong?'

'Nothing that a wise man with a pregnant wife and a house in Sprotbrough should get mixed up in,' she said.

As she strode along the pavement the car went slowly by and Trevor's face turned to watch her. Like a kerb-crawler looking for a pick-up, she thought. It wouldn't surprise her. Yes, it would, she corrected. He hadn't changed *that* much. And on the whole she approved of the changes. On the whole.

But he'd had his warning, and there'd be no more. If he wanted to share her worries that was his business. She didn't want it. She certainly had no intention of sharing his.

12

She was right about having worries enough of her own. At four o'clock in the morning they woke her with a violence so extreme that a physical assault would have been preferable. She was lost in a shell-pocked no-man's-land. Like tracer-shot out of the darkness there came streaming at her thoughts of Sam and her mother and Monk and Ivor and Trevor and a million other concerns, large and small, intimate and universal, till she longed to be back on her island where at least it had seemed that a single step would let her plummet into the quick oblivion of the white sea.

She rose and took three Valium tablets and after the third she looked reflectively for a long time at those that remained in the bottle. The next morning she wondered if she had really been contemplating suicide, but it all seemed so distant and vague that it was as hard to pin down as a childhood memory.

She had slept in and her father had got his own breakfast and gone to work.

Black mark, she thought. Still, it would give Mum something to go on about, perhaps even an extra motive for living. Callous? Not really. Those who survive are those who most want to survive. As for herself, what reason had she for surviving? To look after her father if Mum died? There would be plenty who'd reckon it her duty, especially once the news about Sam got out. Life gave strange choices – a future in Moscow with Sam, or in Doncaster with Ivor! Always supposing Sam, and his Russian masters (or mistresses?) wanted her. Her welcome in Doncaster was more certain, though not, she imagined, in all respects more welcoming. Jennifer Challenger for instance, weighed down with kids, wouldn't be too happy to have a divorced and child-free old flame of Trevor's flickering so close.

Which was worse then, the terror of strangeness or the horror of familiarity?

Danny started barking and a moment later the doorbell rang.

It was Wallace. She didn't ask him in, didn't say anything at all, but just stood looking at him through the narrowly opened door.

'I wondered if you'd like to have lunch with me?'

She shook her head.

'There's someone I'd like you to meet,' he added.

'Let me guess,' she said. 'It's your little crippled daughter who's always worshipped me from afar.'

'It's an American woman called Hibbert. Sally Ann Hibbert.'

He didn't look as if he was observing her closely to check her reaction. But neither did he offer any explanation other than the name.

'Why should I want to meet this woman?' she asked.

'She knew – knows – Sam.'

'Me too,' said Molly. 'And a lot of other people. What's special about this Sally Ann Hibbert?'

'She's mixed up in this business. Will you come?'

'Wait there,' said Molly. She closed the door and looked at the telephone for a moment. Then she went upstairs and put her shoes and a coat on.

They didn't speak until the blue Cortina reached the roundabout by the town racecourse. Wallace sent the car round it three times before pulling out on the road south.

'What's the matter? Are you lost?' demanded Molly.

'Just a trick I picked up from the comic strips,' said Wallace. 'I don't want any gatecrashers.'

'Where are we going, anyway?' asked Molly, suddenly alarmed. 'I have to be back in Doncaster by two o'clock.'

'Not far,' said Wallace. 'It's only eleven.'

Their destination turned out to be a hotel a few miles south of the town. Molly hadn't been there since Trevor had taken her to a dinner-dance when she was twenty. It had seemed pretty posh then. Now it looked merely pretentious.

Wallace collected a key from the receptionist, a bored girl who showed no interest as they mounted the stairs together.

'They probably get a lot of travellers here,' said Wallace, as though catching her thought.

He opened his room and ushered her in.

'Wait there,' he said.

She sat on one of the two chairs the room contained, turning it so it faced the door. She heard Wallace go farther down the corridor and tap gently on another door. There was a brief whispered conversation, then footsteps.

It came as a shock to see how young the woman looked. Molly had been expecting someone the same age as Sam, that is nearly twelve years older than herself. But at first glance this woman looked barely thirty.

A second glance was more reassuring. Her face had that strongly contoured Spanish-American bone structure which is almost ageless as long as too many carbohydrates don't pad out the flesh. But the skin was tightening around the eyes and the mouth and across the wide brow, and the rich blue-blackness of the hair was duller at the roots than it ought to be.

Yes, she could be forty plus, but you'd need a strong hint to put you on the track.

Well, if anyone's had a hint, I have, thought Molly. If Monk was to be believed this woman had lain with her legs apart to let Sam in, and then again to let Sam's child out. Put like that, it didn't sound much to be jealous about. Put like that it sounded too undignified to even contemplate.

'Mrs Keatley,' said the woman in a soft West Coast accent. 'I'm Sally Ann Hibbert. I guess you know something about me.'

'She didn't ask any questions,' said Wallace from the doorway.

'I'd like to talk to you, Miss Hibbert,' said Molly. 'But alone, please.'

'I'm the soul of discretion,' protested Wallace.

'I know all about journalists' discretion,' said Molly. 'It's not the same as trustworthiness. One of us goes.'

'All right,' said Wallace. 'All right. I'll just be down the corridor if you need me.'

'Why should we need him?' wondered Molly as Wallace closed the door.

'I did,' said the other woman.

'So you did,' said Molly. 'This is all very mysterious, Miss Hibbert. Are the police after you?'

The American shook her head.

'I haven't broken any laws, Mrs Keatley. None of your country's anyway.'

'And your own?'

'A few, I guess. Working in government, you sign a paper saying you'll keep your mouth shut.'

'Like the Official Secrets Act?'

'That's right. I didn't keep my mouth shut. I saw Sam's name on a list of people fingered by that defector, Leskov. And I told him.'

'Why should you do that, Miss Hibbert?'

Molly listened to the even, slightly puzzled tone of her voice and felt pleased. After the violent onslaught of the night, she was back together again. On her island, yes, but for the moment safe. She was perhaps being a little too English in response to Sally Ann's American-ness. But that added a certain definition to the role which made it easier to sustain.

She thought of all Sam's mannerisms and assertive prejudices. Were these too merely so much roughage to hold his act together?

'Sam and I were old friends.'

'Old?'

'I did a couple of semesters at Durham way back. We met there.'

'And for the sake of a twenty-year-old memory, you imperilled your job, and possibly your freedom?'

The American had lit a cigarette and was taking such deep puffs that the end glowed cherry-red through the ash.

'You're playing games, Mrs Keatley!' she burst out suddenly. 'Look, I don't want to hurt you, but either all this is . . .'

She tailed off and went back to her cigarette, making a hopeless gesture with her free hand.

'All right,' said Molly. 'I haven't got all day. You were lovers. You had a child. It died. You went back to America. At some point you started a career in whatever you call the diplomatic service over there. Fate brings you back to England. So carry on. I'm agog. I can't put it down.'

94

Sally Ann Hibbert looked at her in bewilderment.

'He never said you were like this,' she said. 'He always said – '

'Forget the dialogue. Just show me the pictures,' said Molly.

The American stubbed out her cigarette and lit another.

'It was about six months ago,' she said. 'We met again by accident. We saw each other a few times. We talked about the old days. That was all. To start with.'

'To start with? You mean you waited for a few days before getting into bed?' said Molly.

'It was a couple of months!' protested Sally Ann Hibbert.

'A couple of months! Oh, the will-power. Oh, the agonies of restraint,' said Molly.

'I'm sorry, but it happened. These things do. To start with, it was just an affair. Then it began to get serious. For me, I mean. I don't know what it meant for Sam. Then about three weeks ago, I saw his name. I shouldn't have seen it, really. That stuff came my way by accident. But there it was. Sam Keatley. I was in a fix. OK, so I would have laid money it was a mistake, but security's like credit-rating, once an error gets into the system, it's hell getting it out. I persuaded myself that Sam had to be told. I didn't come right out with it, I did a bit of fishing first, but he soon caught on. After that there was no going back.'

'And then you realized it was no mistake.'

The American woman sighed deeply.

'Telling him was a mistake, maybe. I never saw him again. I rang him at his office a couple of times, but the defences were up. Then a few days later, he rang me.'

'What day was that?' asked Molly to break the intro-spective silence that followed.

The American looked at her almost mockingly.

'You should know, honey. It'll be red-ringed in your diary too. The day he took off. About ten in the morning he rang me at the Embassy.'

'The Embassy! Wasn't that a bit risky?'

'Why?' said Sally Ann. 'Only the Russians tap our incom-ing lines. He just said something like, *I'm on my way. They'll know you're mixed up in this some way. I hope there's no trouble. I'm sorry.* That was it.'

'He told me he was sorry too,' said Molly bitterly. 'He probably hasn't left the country at all. He's still stuck in a telephone-box somewhere, ringing everyone he knows to say he's sorry!'

Hibbert ignored the gag. Molly felt annoyed. She realized she resented someone else claiming such personal emotional involvement in Sam's disappearance.

'I was in a daze the rest of the day. I expected the questions would start any minute. I thought of going to my boss and telling him everything, but I didn't. You don't, do you? You just keep on trying to pretend that the facts mean something else.'

'I know the feeling,' said Molly. 'Where does Wallace come in?'

'Freddie? He's an old friend. There was a thing between us for a while, before Sam showed up again. We'd stayed friends. He's a useful guy in a tight spot. But I didn't get in touch with him straightaway. I had some leave coming and I asked if I could have it right off. It was a slack time with us, and they didn't mind. I just wanted to sit quiet for a few days, but after a while I began to worry about going back, about what was waiting for me. I'd seen nothing in the papers about Sam yet. I was staying in Wales in an old farmhouse that belongs to some friends and they let me use it when they aren't there. No one knew I was there, so for all I knew, the CIA and Interpol were all running round trying to get a trace on me. It was then I contacted Freddie, asked him to make a few discreet enquiries. I tried to keep it casual, but you know what a nose these press men have. He came hot-footing out to Pembrokeshire. We talked a bit and drank a bit and I guess I was glad to have someone to confide in. Well, he left me there and went back to town. By this time I was over-due back at work, but Freddie said forget it and lie low. A couple of days ago, he turned up again and brought me up here. And here I am.'

Molly contemplated her hands, clasped together on her lap in best prim English spinster style. The broad band of her wedding-ring looked almost out of place in such an arrange-ment of fingers. But it was hers. Sam had given her it. Hib-bert's hands were bare.

She stood up, went to the door and shouted, 'Mr Wallace!'

The journalist appeared almost immediately, with what might have been an ironic smile on his dark face.

'What's this all about, Mr Wallace?' asked Molly. 'Why have you brought me here to meet Miss Hibbert? Or perhaps, as Miss Hibbert has made the longer journey, why have you brought her here to meet me?'

'You're both intimately concerned with the welfare and whereabouts of Sam Keatley,' said Wallace. 'I thought a pooling of information might be useful.'

'Then you're wrong,' said Molly. 'I think I'll skip the lunch and get back to town if you don't mind.'

She saw Wallace shoot a questioning glance at the American who shrugged and gave a minute shake of her head.

'I'll put it another way, Mrs Keatley,' said Wallace. 'I want a story and sooner or later there's going to be a good one here. Miss Hibbert, however, isn't so certain what she wants. On the one hand she sees the danger of what she has done. Her old association with Sam and her more recent errors of judgement have put her in a fair way to being accused, not just of an act of amorous folly, but of being part of the same espionage ring as your husband. She is confused. Her instinct is to go after the man she loves. I've tried to persuade her that this would be stupid but she doesn't think much of my arguments. She does, however, admit two practical considerations. The first is, she doesn't know where he is or how to contact him. The second is, she doesn't know what your intentions are, how you feel now towards Sam; nor, just as important, how he feels towards you. That's really why I've brought her up here. To help her decide what's best to do.'

Molly examined her hands once more. Alongside the wedding-ring was the much finer silver band of her engagement ring. Sam hadn't wanted to bother but Doncaster required both and you do not lightly ignore the rituals of your tribe. She began to smile, at the memory of the ring first of all, then at the wedding, then as other things worth a smile crowded into her mind, she began to laugh and finally stood up, laughing heartily at everything.

'You silly bitch,' she said amiably to the American. 'Go home and get your botty spanked. Mr Wallace, I'll be in the bar. Don't be long, please. I really must get back as soon as possible.'

She stopped laughing as she left the room, but something of her mirth must have remained on her face for the barman took her order with a respondent cheeriness and engaged her in pleasant conversation about the improving weather till Wallace appeared at the door jingling his car keys.

They didn't speak on the way back.

13

The surgeon was prompt for his appointment and after a few moments of the usual infant school headmaster treatment, he made a fair readjustment to a converse of peers.

'Removal of the womb, hysterectomy, should that appear to be our best way forward, is a very simple, almost commonplace, operation these days,' he said. 'In America it's commoner than appendectomy, among women of course.'

'I know it's common,' said Molly. 'And I also know that there's a pretty long queue for it on the National Health. My mother's got in after only two days. So there's more to it than that.'

'You're right, of course. What your mother almost certainly has is a cancer of the body of the womb. This is a bit different from the kind of thing the routine smear test diagnoses. We've no real idea how far this has gone. If, as we hope, it's still confined to the womb itself, then a hysterectomy will suffice and the operation will be no more difficult than in any other case. On the other hand . . .'

'Yes?'

'Well, we won't know till Friday. But there's no point in hanging about. We've got to find out how far things have gone. Your mother was a long time making up her mind to see Dr Lamb.'

'She was frightened,' said Molly. 'If she had told someone earlier . . . But she doesn't talk about personal matters easily, not even to the family.'

'No. That can be frightening too,' said Sterling. 'But she's settled down very well now, I gather. I had a chat with her. She was telling me about your husband. I think I met him once.'

'Really?' said Molly. 'I'd hang on to that. Thanks for seeing me, Mr Sterling.'

I've got to stop being significant, she told herself as she made her way to the ward. I'm scattering dramatic irony like confetti.

Her mother was in a sombre mood, but to Molly's relief the melancholy turned out to be vicarious. The frail old lady had gone for her 'op' and Mrs Haddington's prognosis was not hopeful.

'Heart,' she said, nodding vigorously.

'Is that what's wrong?' asked Molly.

'Oh no. Something about her bladder. But that blueness about the lips, I've seen it before. It's not the operation she's got to worry about, it's the anaesthetic.'

'I'm sure the doctors will take care,' said Molly and when her mother pursed her lips prior to expressing her view of the doctors, she hastily changed the subject by revealing that she'd slept in and thus omitted to make Ivor's breakfast.

That night the skies were clear, but Trevor turned up with his car once more just as they were setting out for the hospital. Molly expressed neither surprise nor gratitude. He had been warned and he'd made up his mind.

Nor did she hesitate later when, after dropping her father at the Club, Trevor suggested they too stopped off for a drink somewhere.

Somewhere turned out to be about fifteen miles east of Doncaster and she noted the way Trevor peered assessingly into the bar before opening the door fully and ushering her in.

'What would you have done if your managing director had been leaning on the bar?' asked Molly as she sipped her Dubonnet.

'Him? Nothing,' said Trevor. 'He knows all about me. Most people do. It was people who might recognize you I was worried about.'

Molly laughed incredulously.

'What's so funny?'

'I don't know. Yes I do. The contrast between you being so smug about your own lecherous reputation and so solicitous about my good name!'

'You think that's incongruous?' asked Trevor.

'As a romantic, I'm touched. As a liberated woman, I'm nauseated.'

'You think you're liberated? We don't have much of that in Sprotbrough. Wife-swapping, yes. Liberation, hardly.'

'I don't know,' said Molly. 'Do *you* think I am?'

'I don't know about liberated. I think you're in some sort of bother.'

'And you'd like to know? You've thought about it, have you?'

He nodded.

'All right,' she said. 'Here it is.'

She watched him closely as she spoke, not certain how she would grade the possible responses, but certain she knew what they might be.

A broad grin, rapidly suppressed, was not one of them.

'What's so funny?' she now asked in her turn.

'I'm sorry. I thought of Carruthers of MI5. You're not Carruthers, are you?'

'I'm empty,' she said, rather annoyed, pushing her glass across the table.

'Dubonnet still? Does this stuff make you drunk?'

'Do you want me drunk?'

'Only if nothing else will do,' he said.

When he returned with the drinks, he said, 'What are you going to do?'

'You don't seem to have any difficulty in believing all this,' said Molly.

'Why? It's not a gag, is it?'

'I don't know what I'm going to do,' said Molly. 'I live from day to day. In a hideous, selfish kind of way, this business of Mum's operation has just come at the right time. Does that revolt you?'

'Not if my being unfaithful to my pregnant wife doesn't revolt you.'

Molly looked at her watch and downed her new drink.

'Time to move,' she said.

'Don't you want another?'

'No need,' she said.

On the way back they stopped in a country lane. The front seats folded almost flat, and making love in a car wasn't anywhere as difficult as she'd always imagined. She gave and received wholeheartedly, doing things that she had never essayed with Sam. It was a wild, exhilarating experience and would have been perfect if she could have fallen quietly asleep afterwards and awoken in her own soft bed.

But putting on proved far more complicated than taking off and when Trevor switched on the courtesy light to assist in the search for their scattered clothes, the steamed-up windows, the confined space, the little bunch of white heather tied round the mirror, the paper handkerchiefs and the liquorice allsorts box in the glove compartment, all scratched away at her sense of pleasure like Danny's claws at a bedroom door.

Trevor lit a cigarette.

'I've often thought of you,' he said.

'That's nice. How many times? Four? Five? In twelve years.'

'No. I mean, when I've done it. When I've been coming, your face has just swum into my mind.'

'Really? And who were you thinking of just now? Jennifer?'

She completed her toilet and stepped out of the car to breathe the fresh night air.

Trevor joined her, leaving the car door wide open.

'She has a good nose, does she?' asked Molly.

He put his arms around her shoulders.

'What *are* you going to do?' he asked.

'I don't know!' she snapped. 'I'm not used to making decisions.'

'Come on!' he said. 'You seem to have been making them pretty effectively since all this happened. A lot of women would just have folded up.'

'No,' she said. 'They haven't been decisions. Time-killers. One foot in front of the other across the desert away from the wreck. Stopping still's a decision. Do you know, I don't think I've really decided anything since I decided to get away from Doncaster. That consumed all my decision-making for the next two or three decades!'

'I'm glad that jilting me took a bit of an effort,' said Trevor. 'Look, it seems to me that, pared down to the bone, the issue's pretty simple. Either you follow Sam and start a new life with him, or you stay here and divorce him. How are you for money?'

'Money! There speaks a Yorkshireman. What's money got to do with anything?'

'Nothing as long as you've got enough to take that high moral tone. Listen. There'll be no more salary. He's not dead, so there'll be no insurance. And even if you divorce him, Moscow's a long way to go to enforce a maintenance order. You could always sell your memoirs, of course. I married a spy. A red in my bed.'

'I must say you've surprised me, Trev,' said Molly. 'You've taken this very coolly.'

'Why shouldn't I? It's done me nothing but good,' he answered. 'I spent three, no, four, of my formative years in which not a day went by without me dreaming of bedding you. You've no idea what it was like – women don't work like that, or at least so I've been led to believe. Lusting all the time, erections in awkward places, nocturnal emissions, masturbatory fantasies. I tried my best, perhaps I should say my hardest, but it got me nowhere. Now after all these years I'm getting everything I dreamt of, and all because your Sam's gone to Moscow! Of course I'm taking it coolly. The only alternative is to jump for joy!'

'I think on the whole,' said Molly slowly, 'that if I set the excess of sexual flattery in that speech against the lack of human sympathy, it's probably a very pretty speech. And I also think that if there'd been any slight sign that you might turn out like this all those years ago, I might have stayed after all. Or left a lot earlier, I don't know which.'

They stood in companionable silence and looked out over the hawthorn hedgerow across the dark fields to where in the distance the lights of a huge power station dimmed the surrounding stars.

Suddenly a brighter, closer light bathed them, sending their shadows leaping across the hedge like spider-men, as bumping up the lane came a car. It stopped a few yards behind Trevor's vehicle and they heard someone get out, though he remained invisible behind the undimmed headlights. Then a figure moved forward.

' 'Evening, sir, madam,' he said. 'This your car?'

It was a policeman. Molly did not know whether to be relieved or alarmed.

'That's right, officer,' said Trevor easily. 'Are we in your way?'

'No, sir,' said the constable. He walked slowly round the car peering through the open doors at the still reclining seats.

'Can I see your licence, sir?' he asked when he got back to his starting-point.

Trevor had it ready.

'Thank you, sir.'

He studied it gravely, then returned it.

'Sorry to have troubled you, sir. Had to take a look, car parked in a lonely spot like this. Will you be staying here long?'

'No. Just going, actually,' said Trevor.

'I'll say good night then,' said the constable. 'Good night, Mr Challenger. Mrs Challenger.'

He returned to his car, the darkness behind the headlights swallowing him like a hole in space.

'Cheeky sod,' said Trevor as the police car reversed to the metalled road. 'What do you think? Coincidence?'

'God knows,' said Molly. 'There are probably people thick enough to think I need watching still. Carruthers of the KGB.'

'They should have asked me,' said Trevor. 'I could have told them you're not Carruthers.'

He turned her towards him and kissed her long and hard.

'Time to go home,' said Molly.

He dropped her at the end of Rothwell Avenue.

'Trevor,' she said. 'Leave me alone. You don't want to get mixed up in this.'

'I thought I'd had my warning,' he said.

'You're getting another chance.'

'I know,' he said. 'I've been taking it.'

'There's nothing in this for either of us,' said Molly. 'I'm just marking time.'

'That's better than the other way round,' said Trevor.

'Oh God. I've got you being smart now!' she said.

'Yes, you have, haven't you?'

*

The next morning Molly managed to get up before Ivor and have his breakfast ready. He ate it in silence and as he went to get his coat he contrived to nudge the knapsack behind the kitchen door. It moved heavily. He made no comment but returned with his donkey-jacket on a moment later and swung the knapsack over his shoulder.

'I'm off then,' he said. 'Back for tea.'

Molly made herself a mug of coffee and poured marmalade on to a hunk of bread. This was her fingerhold on Continental elegance, Sam had mocked. He was like Ivor, a full English breakfast man. Would he get English breakfasts in Russia? She had been washing the dishes that morning when he came back. He hadn't had much of an appetite, she recalled. And the dishes had still been lying in the sink the following morning. That had been a sign. She was a meticulous housekeeper, emphasizing her tidiness to balance Sam's carelessness. But since that day, she had not been able to bother. In fact she had not been able to be most of the things she had been before. Was it all façade, or was this other woman, sharp, untidy, ready to make love on a hearthrug or in a car, the front, as though by such a rapid change she could avoid the pain which the old Molly must have felt?

She finished her coffee, flicked on the radio to let pop-music flood the dark cellars of her mind, and started to wash up. As she was drying, she heard the letter-box flap. A large buff envelope lay on the hall floor. She picked it up and saw that it was addressed to her.

She hefted it in her hand as though by feel and weight she could guess its contents. Then she opened it.

It contained a travel brochure describing the attractions of a seven-day package holiday in Bucharest, documentation indicating that she had booked such a holiday and a plane ticket.

The flight departed from East Midlands Airport at two-thirty p.m. the following day.

14

The frail old lady had survived the operation and after a night's rest was adjudged fit enough to be cross-examined by Mrs Haddington, whose findings were passed on to a group of friends who had arrived for the afternoon visit. The ward sister had weighed up these formidable ladies and wisely decided not to apply the letter of the law, so they all sat around the bed and talked in chorus but with Mrs Haddington's voice indisputably carrying the solo line.

Molly rose some ten minutes before the hour was up and kissed her mother's cheek.

'Off already?' asked one of the visiting party with the ghost of reproach in her voice.

'Yes,' she answered calmly. 'Dad likes a Scotch pie for his tea on Thursday and I'd better get down to Marks' before they get sold out.'

Her mother nodded approval at this flattening formula and as she left Molly heard her interlocutor attempt to re-ingratiate herself by saying, 'She's a good lass.'

'She's always been close to her dad,' said Mrs Haddington. 'Always, from a little girl.'

Did she believe it? wondered Molly as, irritated by the tardiness of the lift, she walked down the stairs. Perhaps this was the blueprint for the successful life – for the first thirty-five to forty years you carved out the future; after that you just chipped away at the past.

In town she bought her father's pie – her mother would check the story tonight – and strolled idly round the streets. Here they had chipped away at the past with a vengeance. Doncaster had never been a beauty spot, but at least it had been homely. The planners and developers had worked at it like a committee of plastic surgeons. Every good intention was marked with a scar.

'Molly, how's your mother?'

It was Jennifer Challenger whom she was passing unnoticed. Her face was slightly flushed and her smile far from beaming. Perhaps she had miscalculated with the make-up, but Molly had a feeling that, had she not by accident ignored Jennifer, then Jennifer would by design have ignored her.

'She's OK, in the circumstances I mean, thanks.'

'That's good,' said Jennifer. There was a hiatus now in which the two women stood on the pavement and looked at each other without speaking, Jennifer with the breathless look of one who is about to speak and Molly (she hoped) with the alert look of one who is eager to listen. Jennifer, she realized, was pretty much a cypher to her, fossilized in her teens and little considered since then. She had had something of a reputation for flightiness, but this was the common lot of any pretty girl not in one's own intimate set. The news of the engagement between Jennifer and Trevor had come as a surprise, momentarily even a shock, but thereafter she had mentally covered them with leaves and left them to sleep time away like the Babes in the Wood. But it had been babes in the womb instead, and just as Trevor had grown and changed so must this woman who now confronted her on the edge of the busy street.

For it was a confrontation, she realized. Or would be if she permitted it.

'I'm afraid Trevor won't be able to take you to the hospital tonight,' resumed Jennifer. 'We're having some people round to dinner. But it's not far to walk, is it?'

'Not far,' agreed Molly. 'And I've been lucky to have him twice.'

She intended no double entendre or at least not consciously. Was her intonation suggestive? She thought not but could not swear to it.

'I expect Sam will be coming up as soon as he can,' said Jennifer shrilly. Was *that* last clause over-emphasized?

'I expect so.'

'You must bring him round to see us. If he wouldn't mind an evening with ordinary people and their noisy kids, that is. I'd really like to meet him.'

'Haven't you met Sam?' asked Molly, pretending surprise.

'We said hello once. No, you've got an advantage over me there. It's only right we should even the balance, isn't it?'

She laughed unconvincingly. No, not unconvincingly. Threateningly and with conviction.

Molly was surprised to find herself tempted to push things a few steps further, see how far the other woman would go. But she resisted easily. There wasn't much point in provoking a fight for something she did not at the moment want to win. So she said an abrupt goodbye and strode quickly away. But as she sat on the homeward bus she realized that she was in fact disappointed that she wouldn't be seeing Trevor that night. It wasn't sexual disappointment, she analysed, rather the simple human need for a *confidant*. What she really wanted (so she reassured herself) was someone with whom she could discuss the mystery of the Rumanian holiday. Sam must be responsible for having the flight booked, of that she was sure. Perhaps he was insisting that he should see her before he appeared in public. Or perhaps one of his masters thought it would be a good idea to have Mrs Keatley behind the Curtain when the news broke. Whatever the idea, this seemed a simple, anonymous way of doing it – a provincial airport, a package tour – she could be drinking *tuica* before Monk knew she'd gone.

Monk. She was assuming that, if he wanted to, he could stop her from leaving the country. On what grounds? she asked herself. This was the very mythology of espionage, the belief in secret police and powers beyond the law, whereas probably the reality behind Monk's weary, wayworn clerk-of-works expression was as commonplace as the man himself.

She corrected herself. Not commonplace. That was a façade too. She was becoming an expert on façades. Perhaps beneath Monk's there lay the kind of man she really wanted to confide in. Knowledgeable, sympathetic, paternal. Why paternal? – he was no older than Sam. She found herself suddenly eager to feel his comforting arm round her shoulder, to smell the fresh-scrubbed soapy smell of him. He would know what to do.

Then with an equally sudden reversal of feeling, she laughed cynically at the prospect. Monk was like an onion and just because she'd penetrated the outer skin she was imagining she'd reached the centre.

But she might as well phone him. There was no point in keeping this from him since she didn't really have to decide whether or not to go. Her mother was being operated on to-morrow and nothing at the end of her journey could justify her absence on such a day.

Yet when she got through, she found herself telling him not about the package through the post, but about Wallace and Sally Ann Hibbert.

'This was yesterday. You've taken your time, missus,' he reproached her.

'Yes. I know. It slipped my mind. I've been busy. Though doubtless,' she added bitterly, recalling the police car in the country lane, 'doubtless you know all about that.'

He did not comment.

'Anything else?' he said.

'Should there be? What about you? Is there anything more about Sam?'

'No, missus. They're keeping him under wraps, wherever he is. Llewellyn's getting the treatment though, which is strange. They must be hard up!'

'What treatment?'

'He's been giving a press conference this afternoon. It'll be in the papers tonight.'

'Is that significant?'

'You tell me, missus. How's your mother?'

'As well as can be expected. They're operating tomorrow.'

'I hope she'll be all right,' said Monk. 'How about you?'

'I hope she'll be all right too,' said Molly.

'In yourself, I mean. You've had a lot to put up with.'

Molly began to cry. Her voice remained unchanged, calm and controlled, but as she replied tears began to run down her cheeks, two steady streams which did not feel as if they had anything to do with her body.

'I'm all right,' she said. 'It's good of you to ask.'

She meant it. She felt that somehow Monk knew she was crying but was too diplomatic to mention it, though why she should credit him with such sensitivity she did not know.

'Thanks for ringing,' said Monk. 'Keep eating the Irish Stew. Ta-ta.'

As abruptly as they had started the tears stopped. Molly washed her face, then sat down in the living-room and took the travel documents from the old bureau by her father's chair. She should have told Monk. She had meant to tell Monk. But she hadn't been able to. She tried to work out why with something of the objective interest of a botanist examining a new plant form.

After a while she thought she had it.

They were from Sam, a gesture, an invitation, perhaps the only one she would ever get from the new Sam, certainly the only private one, for the spotlight of publicity burns as it illumines and the blisters are still painful though the darkness returns. Not to go now might mean never to go, a betrayal more brutal and lasting than anything she had done with Trevor in the car last night. But she couldn't go. Not till it was all over with her mother. She realized suddenly but without shock that she was convinced her mother would die. Not tomorrow perhaps, but soon. She would lie in her hospital bed, strong, and domineering, and refusing to admit the truth, while half a dozen frail old ladies came and were cured and departed, till finally she too would depart and her daughter and her husband would return to the empty house sharing that sense, both active and passive, of betrayal which grips the bereaved heart like a band of mourning crape.

So, stay she must. There were words to speak which at least might cut her free from Sam for ever. Now they might not be spoken and perhaps for ever his face would haunt her moments of greatest joy as Trevor claimed her face had haunted his.

But at least she would not have told Monk.

15

'Next time you see me I'll be on the mend,' said Mrs Haddington as the end-of-visiting bell sounded.

'Yes, Mum,' said Molly.

'What are you staring at, lass?' her mother asked irritably. 'Have I got a dirty face or something?'

'No. I'm sorry. I didn't mean to stare.'

In fact she couldn't keep her eyes off her mother's face. Her father on the other hand didn't seem able to look his wife straight in the eyes. He had wandered round the room, peered out of the window, examined the flowers, and when he was finally commanded to stop fidgeting and get sat down, he contemplated the coverlet on the bed as studiously as if it had been a Gobelin tapestry.

'I don't know what's up with you two tonight,' Mrs Haddington had expostulated at, one point. 'You've not broken something, have you? Molly, you've not been using my Queen Anne china?'

After that the two of them had made an effort to naturalize their manner, but they made a despondent pair as they walked away from the hospital.

Almost opposite the entrance to the hospital was a pub, a large roadhouse whose clientele and beer Ivor Haddington affected to despise.

'Come on, I'll buy you a drink,' said Molly.

'In yon place?' said Ivor.

'It's my money,' said Molly. 'Come on.'

They sat and drank in silence, melancholy on Molly's part, suspicious on Ivor's as he supped his pint like a Sultan's gustator.

'She'll be all right,' he said finally.

'I'm sure,' said Molly.

'It preys on your mind, even when you're not thinking

of it,' said Ivor. 'I dreamt the other night . . .'

'Yes?'

'I dreamt your mother were dead.'

'Oh yes?' said Molly, trying to keep the tone light. 'What did you do?'

He shot her a glance, shamefaced yet with an undershadow of defiant humour.

'I got a pair of pigeons,' he said.

Molly looked at him reproachfully. They both began to grin. Finally they laughed out loud.

'Let's have t'other half,' said Ivor, finishing his pint.

'All right,' said Molly.

But it was only a temporary lightening and they were as silent as before by the time they opened the front door and Danny-boy peered cautiously out of the kitchen before rushing to greet them with a joyful bark.

'He needs a walk,' said Ivor. 'His routine's broke.'

'Shall I take him?' asked Molly.

'No. You make us a cup of something hot. I'll give him a quick run round the block. It'll mebbe blow some of the cobwebs off me too.'

She'd hardly had time to put the kettle on the gas ring when the doorbell rang. Molly opened the door, expecting some neighbour enquiring after her mother's health. On the doorstep stood Wallace. By his side, slouched against the wall, was Sally Ann Hibbert.

' 'Evening,' said Wallace. 'May we come in?'

There was a strong smell of Scotch, whether from one or both it was hard to tell. Wallace looked all right, but it might be just the façade of practice. The American woman looked far from all right as she glowered sullenly at Molly, who was pleased to discover no difficulty tonight in believing she was in her forties.

'Just for a moment,' urged Wallace. 'It'll be better. The neighbours.'

'Not again,' said Molly. 'You lot use the neighbours like Genghis Khan used his Horde.'

'You lot? Which lot is that?' asked Wallace.

'Bullies.'

'I'm sorry. I don't mean to sound bullying. I just thought . . .'

He flickered his eyes significantly towards Hibbert, whether in appeal or additional threat Molly did not know. But she said, 'All right. Just for a minute. My father will be back shortly.'

That information was probably redundant, she thought as she led them into the living-room. Doubtless Wallace had seen her father leave. And Danny too; he would have been glad to see Danny go!

'What do you want?' she asked.

'You bitch,' said the woman thickly. 'You turned me in.'

'I did what?'

'Don't try to deny it! You rang the cops. You goddamn jealous cow!'

She spat the words out with a fury that made her tremble. Molly looked enquiringly at Wallace.

'Sally Ann had visitors at the hotel,' he said. 'A couple of fellows from the Embassy.'

'So?'

'They implied they'd got their information from you.'

Molly shrugged.

'So what?' she said. 'They didn't, not directly. But what's her problem anyway? She's still at large.'

'And I'm still in the room, for Christ's sake! Don't talk about me as if I'm not here!'

'It's called wishful thinking,' said Molly. 'Mr Wallace, I take it you've got something else on your mind besides having me yelled at?'

The journalist nodded.

'You won't believe me, but it's your welfare I've got on my mind. No, I'm not claiming pure altruism, Mrs Keatley. It's just a happy coincidence – my story and your welfare come in the same packet.'

For a second Molly wondered if this was a kind of pun and glanced uneasily towards the bureau. But it was absurd. Wallace couldn't possibly know about the packet she'd received that morning.

'What's changed since last we met, apart from Miss Hibbert's career prospects?' asked Molly.

'A defector called Llewellyn gave a press conference in Moscow today. You've probably read about him.'

Molly kept her expression neutral.

'So?'

'So several things. I think there may be a connection between Llewellyn's taking off and your husband's disappearance. So does my editor. More important, though, is the line he's planning to take on Llewellyn. You see, what the Russians have done is very clever. Instead of trying to project Llewellyn as the biggest thing since Fuchs, they're concentrating on his relative *unimportance*. He stood up at the conference and told the audience precisely what he'd been working on. Basically what it comes down to is fuel economy – giving strike aircraft longer range without loss of efficiency.'

'He should have defected to General Motors,' said Molly.

'I gather it's a bit more complicated than I've made it,' said Wallace, gladly taking the chance to smile. 'There was a fifteen-page hand-out allegedly giving all the details. It looks real enough. Next came a bit of the old moral line, universality of science, etcetera. Applause from the Eastern Bloc press. So far, it's the usual stuff. Then comes question time and the first guy up, obviously carefully primed, asks Llewellyn if he really believes he can justify selling his country's secrets to an enemy power. Llewellyn looks surprised. What secrets? he asks. I've sold no secrets. First, I got no money for what I did. It was purely a matter of conscience. Second, I didn't have any secrets to sell.'

'I don't follow,' said Molly. 'And I'm not much bothered. What's all this fiddle got to do with Sam?'

'Hang about,' said Wallace. 'Now another hand-out is passed round. This one gives details of work the Americans are doing on a similar project – only it's a couple of stages advanced beyond the British version! And finally a third hand-out is produced – this one consisting of offprints, with translation, of articles describing parallel research which has allegedly been published in a couple of freely available Russian scientific journals!'

'Great,' said Molly, yawning.

'Don't you see? At a stroke, they've shown that one NATO hand doesn't know what the other's doing and that they're both wasting public money in any case! And Llewellyn is set up as the lily-white boy, following his conscience without harming his country!'

Wallace seemed really delighted at this piece of Kremlin cleverness, thought Molly. Perhaps he fancied himself as a bit of a puppet-master and was impressed by such a prime example of his art.

'I still don't know what it's got to do with me,' she said.

'It's like this,' he said. 'Basically, my editor wants to go along with this line. We feel that the UK is wasting millions of pounds in the Defence budget, not just in an effort to keep up with the Russians, but in direct competition with her own so-called allies. Unless there's some real co-operation in NATO – behind-the-scenes co-operation, not just playing soldiers in the snow now and then – they might as well pack up their cardboard forts and go home.'

'So you want to use Llewellyn's press conference to strengthen NATO?' said Molly, raising her eyebrows. 'Hardly the Russian aim, I should have thought.'

'Isn't there a drink in this place, for God's sake?' said Sally Ann Hibbert, who had collapsed in a chair and looked as if she might soon be sick.

Wallace ignored her.

'No, of course not. Next on the menu we reckon will be Sam. He'll come across as strong as Llewellyn came weak. Llewellyn will have got people wondering just why the hell we're paying so much money to "discover" stuff the Yanks and the Russians have had for years; now Sam will convince the Americans that they're dead right not to share research findings with the Europeans whose security is so obviously lousy. So – the NATO countries will be stirred up at every level, from little tax-payer to big policy-maker.'

Hibbert rose unsteadily.

'I need a drink,' she announced and when Molly made an uncertain move, she was waved away imperiously.

'I'll get it,' said the American. 'Water. Drink of water.'

'She'll be all right,' said Wallace as Sally Ann went through the door with the exaggerated steadiness of the stoned. 'Mrs Keatley, has Sam been in touch with you?'

Surprised by the directness of the question, Molly shook her head.

'I don't really believe you,' said Wallace. 'But it doesn't matter if he hasn't. He will be. When he does, I want you to put me in touch with him.'

'You'll get your chance at his press conference, Mr Wallace,' said Molly. 'I presume they'll let him have a press conference?'

'You can bet on it. No, I've got to talk to him before that. I've got a proposition to put to him.'

'You want him for your ice-hockey correspondent,' suggested Molly.

'It'll be good for him, it'll be good for you. Yes, don't say it. It'll be good for me too. Here's how it goes. He sells us his story. Hang on a minute, let me finish. What we really want are as many examples as he can produce of the kind of thing we've had from Llewellyn – duplication of effort, wasting tax-payers' money etcetera. The inefficiency of our security systems won't come amiss either. We already know that his name was revealed via Leskov, but the Americans had Leskov for over three months before they condescended to pass on the information. We've no intention of glorifying what Sam's done, let me make that clear. But we would present the fairest picture we could.'

'And you think he'd give a damn about that?' asked Molly.

'We all like to justify ourselves to those we betray, Mrs Keatley,' said Wallace seriously. 'Which is why I'm sure he'll want to see you. Look, I'm sure I can sell it to him if only I can talk to him, preferably before he's put on display. I don't think his masters would object, either – it's one of those rare occasions when two opposing goals can apparently be reached by a common route.'

'And how does this turn out good for me?' asked Molly.

'Two ways. One, you'll need money. We'll pay *you* for the story Sam gives us. That should please him and save us the embarrassment of paying cash direct to a defector. Two, we'll put you and your family under exclusive contract for your own stories. Don't get angry! Once this breaks, the popular press'll be on your back till you either crack up or sign up. A contract with us would stop the pestering, and knowing our legal department was on the watch would make them think twice about having a go at you by innuendo. You wouldn't have to write a thing, though if you cared to take up the offer in, say, the next six months, that'd be fine. Look, don't say anything now, Mrs Keatley. Think about it. All I want is a chance to contact Sam.'

There was a distant crash and a cry of anger or pain. Sally Ann Hibbert appeared a moment later. In her right hand she held the razor-edged carving knife, and she was sucking at the index finger of her left.

'What kind of place is this?' she said. 'They've even got fog indoors.'

Her teeth were bloodstained from a cut on her finger. With her jet black hair and drink-pale face she looked like the newest recruit in a vampire film. Molly pushed by her and went into the kitchen, where she discovered that the kettle she had put on in preparation for her father's return had almost boiled dry. She switched off the gas and opened the window to let the steam out.

'I thought I'd have a sandwich, soak up some of the booze. OK?'

The American was behind her, more gothic still in the steam-filled air. A loaf of bread lay on the kitchen table with a blood-stained slice half detached.

'Make yourself at home,' said Molly. 'How's your finger?'

'I'll live. Listen. Are you going to play along with Fred?'

'Where do you come into it?' asked Molly. It was a question she'd want Wallace to answer too.

'I don't come in. I'm in,' said Sally Ann. 'I want a chance at Sam too. I figure I've earned it.'

'*Earned!*' said Molly. 'For what? A couple of lays in twenty-year instalments. You must be the first HP whore.'

Sober and beautiful, drunk and ugly, this woman makes me jealous, she thought. It's incredible, everything else, and I've got to be jealous too!

'My career's gone bust! They can jail me if they want, do you know that? I've given up more for Sam in a couple of weeks than you had to give up after eight bloody years!'

She was yelling at the top of her voice and waving the carving knife in slashing, emphatic gestures. Molly had forgotten how drunk she was. Perhaps more than drunk. Her nerves were clearly wound up to breaking-point and Molly could only guess what pharmaceutical flotsam and jetsam might be bobbing around in a sea of whisky.

'All right,' she said in a conciliatory tone. 'Let's talk it over with Fred.'

She tried to walk by the American but felt her cardigan grasped and next moment was pushed so hard against the cooker, the gas rings rattled.

'Fuck Fred! This is for us.'

The words were slurred, the breath close to her cheek damp and hot and reeking of Scotch.

'Understand me, Mrs Keatley. I've got a story too and it'll make better reading than anything you can tell. Who's bothered about a frigid wife when there's a hot mistress telling how it really was? I'm going to get something out of this mess even if it's only money!'

Here then was the reason that Wallace had brought her. Another threat. Tell the neighbours, tell the world. Journalists were tarts, publicity was their sex, and they used it both as goods and as weapon. Anger surged in her mind, making her forget her policy of conciliation. She tried to wrench free from Sally Ann's grip and when the American pushed her back against the oven once more, she lost her temper and lashed out with her foot.

This did the trick. Her face twisted with pain from the blow to her shin, Hibbert hopped back.

'You cow!' she said, looking at her injured leg. There was a cut on the shin and blood was oozing through the pale brown sheen of her tights.

Molly had time to start feeling apologetic before the knife came swinging at her head. She ducked instinctively, then slid to the floor and rolled away, still not able to believe what was happening even as the American, her face contorted with what could have been anger or despair, pursued her with wild slashing blows.

There wasn't far to roll. As she hit the foot of the kitchen door, she thrust herself into reverse like a swimmer doing a kick turn and, risking the momentary total exposure of her back, she grasped the other woman round the knees and wrestled her to the floor. There was a clang as Sally Ann flung her arms out for support and hit the washing machine. The knife twisted in her grip, then went scuttering away across the tiled floor and disappeared beneath the fridge.

This time Molly's relief was even shorter-lived than her earlier feeling of apology. Her hair was seized, her head forced back till her neck was taut and her mouth opened in a scream which her contorted throat muscles wouldn't let out. She thrust her left hand at Hibbert's face, clawing for the eyes while with the right she pummelled the American's bosom. It was like punching a pillow but it must have been painful, or perhaps fear of blindness did the trick, but her hair was released. Now the woman's arms went round her in a bear-hug and they rolled over and over like lovers, the flushed Red Indian face as close to hers as passion could demand, but butting not kissing, and the teeth which tried to close on her neck were not offering a love-bite but trying to rip flesh from her windpipe.

She shouted now, not a scream of panic, but a cry to Wallace for help. Surely he must have heard? For God's sake, what was the man doing?

Then he was there, dragging the American to her feet and simply by gripping her wrists reducing her murderous fury to an impotent struggling.

These men, thought Molly bitterly. No wonder they think they rule by divine right.

She stood up, drawing in long deep draughts of air. The American looked infuriatingly relaxed, or rather slack, as though something had been cut. Wallace decided it was safe to release one of her wrists and he put out his hand to touch Molly's forearm, standing between them like a referee waiting for the judge's decision.

'What the hell's going on?' he demanded.

'Just get her out of here,' gasped Molly. 'Get her out!'

She had no time, even if she had had any desire, for explanation. Her father would be back any minute. In fact he was overdue. He might well have caught her in mid-struggle on the kitchen floor! She felt sick at the thought. This was no time to involve him in troubles other than those which now must be weighing on his shoulders like a hod of bricks.

'She's ill, you know, not herself. There's a strain, well, you will know . . .'

'Get out! For Christ's sake, can't you understand English! Now! Get out!'

'OK. OK. Sorry. I'll be in touch.'

Molly was in her bedroom before the front door shut behind them. The kitchen bore little mark of the struggle, but her own person was a different matter. Her hair was dishevelled, her right cheek scratched and she had unbeknowings sprained her left thumb and it was already beginning to swell painfully. But most disturbing of all was the discovery that her cardigan was severed beneath the arm, right down to the bottom hem. Nor was it a ragged tear such as might have been caused by main force alone. The thin wool had been cleanly cut. She had not realized how close the carving knife had come.

Quickly she got to work with powder and comb and was just slipping into another cardigan when she heard the front door open and Danny's homecoming bark.

She went into the bathroom and held her thumb under the cold tap for a minute. It helped a little but not much.

Downstairs she found her father in the living-room.

'No tea?' he said reproachfully.

'Sorry. You were a long time.'

'Aye. I met old Bartlett. You know how he goes on. Thinking of going on a trip?'

He was standing by the bureau and now she realized with a shock that he had the travel agent's packet in his hand.

'I thought I might pop across to see Sam for a couple of days,' she said lightly. 'But that'll have to wait till Mum's on the mend. I'll get that tea.'

'Right,' he said, his face sombre at the mention of his wife.

Molly watched till he dropped the packet back into the drawer, then went into the kitchen. She had been silly to leave it where her father might so easily come across it.

Then as she tried to pick up the kettle in her left hand, the pain reminded her that Wallace had been alone in the living-room for several minutes while the great battle was going on.

Had her father's attention been attracted to the packet by finding the bureau drawer open?

She found she didn't much care and set about making the tea.

16

'What've you done to your thumb?' asked Monk.

'I had a little accident.'

'Same accident as scratched your face?' said Monk.

'Same one.'

'I'd watch that, missus. Accidents in the home can be nasty.'

'Fatal, you mean?'

'Oh, nastier than that, missus.'

Her mother's operation was scheduled for two o'clock. Ivor had taken the day off work but had risen even earlier than usual and wandered round the house, disruptive as a poltergeist, till midway through the morning Molly had sent him into town with a long and mainly redundant shopping list. Ten minutes after his departure, Monk had appeared.

'Still watching me?' she said.

He shook his head.

'No. But the Yanks are watching Hibbert,' he said. 'Sooner or later they'll want our help, so they're being all co-operative. What did they want?'

Molly saw no reason not to tell him, omitting only details of the fight (which he probably guessed at) and, once again, the packet (which it wouldn't surprise her if he knew all about anyway).

'But what did they really want?' he wondered when she'd finished.

'Why not what they said?' asked Molly.

'A scoop? Lovers' meeting? Aye, why not, missus? This work turns you suspicious.'

'Was what he said about Llewellyn true?'

'Oh yes. Don't you read the papers?'

'I haven't looked this morning.'

She picked up the tabloid with which she had tried (in vain) to occupy Ivor for more than two minutes. The front page was concerned with the first major football riot of the season. She finally found a couple of paragraphs sandwiched between the air traffic controllers' strike and a naked woman eating a peach, alleged to be symbolic of Harvest Home.

'It gets a better run in some of the others,' said Monk.

'Including Wallace's?'

'Half a page. There's no getting away from it, they're not daft in the Kremlin, missus. Us, we get a nonentity like Llewellyn coming over, we'd tuck him quietly away somewhere. They make his unimportance work for them!'

'Like the Americans letting Hibbert roam loose,' said Molly.

Monk looked at her sharply.

'You're not daft either, missus. She's either what she says she is, gabby in bed – in which case, there's not much point in taking her in; or she's something more – in which case she might lead them somewhere.'

'But they interviewed her in the hotel. She knows they're on to her.'

'But they've played it so they hope she'll reckon they believe her story – if it's not true, that is!'

'And so that she'll reckon they don't believe it if it is true?'

'Same result,' said Monk. 'We'll make an agent of you yet.'

The words were uttered in his normal plainsong, but the rhythmic line must have been subtly altered for they hung in the air like an invitation, or a threat.

'No, you won't, Mr Monk,' said Molly seriously.

'How's your mother?' he replied.

Molly explained how her mother was and Monk nodded with the unresentful cynicism of one who knows that whatever awaits us is always the worst.

'Have you told the doctor anything of your own position?' he asked.

'No. Why should I?'

'Strain,' he said bluntly. 'It's no cakewalk, what you've been going through. He might be able to help you bear up. Or at least know what it's all about if you crack up.'

Molly laughed and wondered if Monk intended his pessimism to be cheering.

'As far as I can make out,' she said, 'Doncaster's jammed full of people who know more about my life than I do myself. And there's so many people watching me, if I jumped off St George's, I'd land soft.'

'Don't bet on it,' said Monk. 'I hope your mam turns out all right.'

He rose to go.

'Won't you have a cup of tea or something?' asked Molly. She didn't want him to go, she realized. She'd have to watch this. She reminded herself that, for all his expressions of sympathetic interest, his real purpose in seeing her was to find new ways of harming her husband.

Yet still she didn't want him to go.

'No, thanks,' he said. 'Your dad'll be back before long and I've work to do anyway. But we'll keep in touch.'

As if taking him literally, she offered her hand at the door. He shook it formally and left. Danny, who had been sticking close to Monk since his arrival letting out little sighs of adoration, now whimpered piteously as she closed the door.

'It's no good, Danny,' said Molly seriously. 'You'll just have to learn like me – from now on, you're on your own.'

The dog barked, jumped up and started licking her face. He obviously didn't believe it. She wondered if she did.

After standing there suffering Danny's embrace and wondering for a few moments if there was anyone she ought to, or would like to, or felt able to ring, she decided she believed it all right, and went into the kitchen to make some coffee.

She was drinking it in the living-room when the phone and the doorbell rang together. She recognized Trevor's figure through the frosted glass instantly, opened the door and without saying anything to him picked up the phone.

'You bitch. You fucking stinking crawling bitch.'

It was a woman's voice, thick with rage and hate and perhaps drink. Her first thought was Hibbert. But there was nothing of America in the intonations.

'Whore! What do you charge in a car? More than against a lamp-post? You cow!'

Horrified, Molly looked into Trevor's face. He looked at her anxiously, lovingly. Possessively.

'Oh, you stupid bastard,' she said and slowly lowered the

receiver so that the tiny, tinny voice was clearly audible between them till she put it on the rest.

'There was no other way,' said Trevor. 'I had to tell her about us.'

He looked pleadingly, anxiously, into her face. But, like the after-taste of a cheap sherry, there was something of smug triumph there too.

'Tell her *what* about us? What the hell is there to tell anyone about us?' demanded Molly.

'That we love each other.'

'Do we? Who says? Have you got it in writing? Has there been a plebiscite or something?'

She was talking with the kind of breathless exhilaration that one feels in a rising gale. There were blasts of anger there, and resentment, and indignation, and grief, and despair, and Trevor had little enough to do with most of them. But when the storm breaks, anyone foolish enough to be caught without shelter must bear the full onslaught.

'The other night, we talked . . . I said . . .'

'I said, you said. The other night. In the car. On the hearthrug. Once, twice. Like a whore. Jennifer's right, like a whore. You don't tell your wife about a whore! No man tells his wife about a whore!'

'Why are you talking like this?' he demanded. 'What's got into you? Molly, I'm telling you, I've left my wife, I want to marry you.'

He reached out and put his hands on her shoulders but she twisted out of the grip and strode into the living-room.

'Marry me, Trev? You're married already! Have you forgotten? Me too, I'm married too. Don't forget that. What makes you think I'd want to marry you anyway? I didn't want to twelve years ago, did I? I thought I made that pretty clear. So what's changed since?'

'I've changed,' said Trevor. 'You've changed. The whole damned world's changed!'

There was a lull in the storm.

'Yes,' she said thoughtfully. 'Yes. The whole world.'

'Molly, I've never stopped thinking of you,' he resumed, eager to press what must have looked like an advantage.

'Yes, you told me,' she answered with a humourless laugh.

'All this time and I've never been out of your masturbatory fantasies! Well, I'm out of them now, duckie, and I'm flattered you're so keen on the real thing. Play your cards right and you could have had your hand in the candy jar for number three. Every good boy deserves a treat. But greedy Trev wants the whole stinking sweet shop! For God's sake, Trevor, what the hell were you thinking of? You've got a couple of kids, another on the way. You know how I'm fixed at the moment. What were you thinking of!'

He stood silent before her, torn between anger and hurt. She waited for the choice, indifferent to either. Violence or pathos, she had reserves of scorn and bitterness and hysteria which could deal with all his weapons.

But suddenly he undermined her with the one weapon she wasn't ready for.

He grinned sheepishly and said, 'You scratched my back the other night. Jennifer didn't notice it till this morning. But she's suspected something's going on. There've been little niggling remarks about you, and last night we had some people round and Jennifer brought you up again. It was pretty vicious stuff and I started defending you, which was what she wanted, I suppose. We had a row, slept apart, but I had to go into our bedroom to get dressed. I thought she was asleep but she wasn't. She noticed the scratches, and it all started again. This time everything came out. I'm sorry.'

Molly shook her head in disbelief.

'So you storm out of the house and she hits the bottle. Jesus! Couldn't you have told her you did it brambling or something?'

'It's no joke, Molly,' he said. 'I mean it. It's you I want. I don't know if I'm ever going to be able to have you, but I know I'll always want you. I wanted you all those years ago, and now I see what you've become, I realize how right I was then. I've been thinking hard about you for the past couple of days – not just erotic fantasies either. When Jennifer started accusing me this morning, I made no attempt to deny it. The opportunity just seemed too good. I'd never do it cold, leave her, I mean. It's a rotten thing to do, more rotten than I could manage in cold blood. I'm not that kind of hard bastard. But I am the kind of soft bastard that will take a comparatively easy way out if it's offered. You ought to know that about me.'

'I always have,' said Molly. 'Oh Trevor, Trevor, what do you want me to do or say?'

'That you'll come away with me. That you love me.'

'I hate people who answer rhetorical questions,' said Molly. 'But since you've been specific, I'll be specific too. No, I won't come away with you. No, I can't honestly say that I love you. Now, don't look hurt. You managed to skip that before and it's always been your least attractive expression. Do I sound hard? I sound hard to myself, but while I think I'm probably able to be a much harder bastard than you (somewhat to my surprise), in this case all it means is that I don't have a problem. Or rather, this problem is one of the few that I don't have. What I mean to say, Trev darling, my sweet loving Trev – no, I'm not saying I love you after all, so don't look so doggishly hopeful, which has always been one of your most attractive expressions – what I mean is, there's no way I can go away with you at the moment, even if I wanted, just as there's no way I can know if I love you, even if I do. I'm as full as a puddle in autumn, and as murky. When I walk, I slosh fears and uncertainties and nightmares through my ears and eyes and mouth. I don't know when I shall be clear and level again but till then I've no problem in telling you what to do.'

'And what's that?' asked Trevor.

In the hall the phone started ringing again.

'That's probably Jennifer looking for round two,' said Molly. 'Go home, Trev. Tell her it was a bramblebush. She won't believe you but if she's got any sense she won't say so.'

'And you?'

'I'll just slosh on till I'm all spilt or I dry up.'

'And then?'

'Who knows?' said Molly. 'God. I feel theatrical!'

'I may not be able to manage it again,' said Trevor seriously. 'Next time it'll take a hard bastard even to be a soft bastard.'

'Next time perhaps I'll come looking for you,' said Molly.

As she closed the front door behind him, the phone stopped ringing. She took it off the hook and sat on the floor next to Danny-boy till her father came home.

17

'I wish Sam were here,' said Ivor suddenly.

Molly almost told him then. They had been sitting in the hospital waiting-room for two hours that seemed like ten and conversation had not flowed. It was as if the anaesthetic which had been pumped into Mrs Haddington had produced a sympathetic reaction.

'There's nothing he could do,' said Molly.

'He gets on well with your mam,' said Ivor. 'And he gets things done.'

'Haven't I got things done?' protested Molly.

'Aye, but up here they pay more heed to a man. And truth is, since this business of your mother started, I've not been much good. No, I haven't. It's knocked the stuffing out of me somehow.'

He sounded as near to tears as Molly had ever known him. The cigarette in his brown-stained fingers had burnt down almost to the knuckles which arthritis had swollen like oak-apples, but he did not feel the heat.

In a desperate effort at diversion, Molly said, 'Sam would be here if he could.'

'Down at the Club once this fellow were going on about the blacks and Sam put him right. He knew his stuff and he could put it across, that's the secret,' continued Ivor. 'That's education. You got yourself a good man there.'

'I'll go and see if there's any news,' said Molly.

She went out and walked along the corridor. The nurse sitting at the desk in the open office at the end of the corridor looked up and shook her head. Molly kept going and when she reached the door which led to the stairway, she turned into it and began to descend. Down and round she went, down and round till she reached the foyer which with its bookstands and flower shop and rows of padded seats looked more like an airport lounge than the entrance to a hospital. But it was not an inapt likeness, she thought. Arrivals and departures. Mrs Haddington will soon be taking off from Ward Twenty. Mr and Mrs Challenger's new baby is expected to land shortly in Ward Five. She walked swiftly across the carpeted floor and went out into the fresh air.

The sun was shining though the wind was chill and for a moment the simple act of stepping out of the hospital into this pattern of dappling light and shifting air was enough to lift her spirits. But only for a moment.

Out loud she said, amazed at the revelation, 'I can imagine no possible good.'

A man going into the hospital glanced enquiringly at her, then passed by. She was unbothered by him, taken up wholly with this startling new discovery. New? Hardly. Surely this was as old as religion. This was the sin against the Holy Ghost, the unforgivable sin. She had never understood that before but she understood it now. This was a long, long step beyond the blackest of subjective depressions. This was the certainty of the human pain and divine indifference. Compared with this, atheism was a peccadillo.

She went back into the building and, ignoring the lifts, once more remounted the stairs. When she reached her landing, she paused and looked out of the tall churchlike window. She could see a long way and very clearly. Doncaster was not a beautiful town, but what signified beauty? Here she had been born, but why be sentimental about the scene of a disaster? Far below cars moved silently along endless roads. People walked and talked and went about their dismal business, ignorant that they were so observed. She neither envied nor pitied them. It was enough that they shared a common doom.

So this was accidie, this was despair, she told herself curiously. It was not the black land she had imagined. It was more like stepping through the looking-glass, and realizing just how fast the human race had to run to keep on the same spot, and knowing it wasn't worth it. A starling darted past the window. She reached out and touched the glass. So a bird could fly. So what? Human beings had a greater strength than that. They could fall.

But not through this window, for there was no way of opening it. No hurry. There would be a time. She was beyond desire, beyond hope and, best of all, beyond pain. Sam. Trevor. Her mother. They had no power now to hurt her, come what may.

And she returned to the waiting-room and discovered Sterling, the surgeon, talking to her father whose chalky face, streaked at last with tears, told her the worst, she was so content to find her new invulnerability proven that she scarcely listened to what Sterling was saying.

In the end it was her father who broke through to her.

'She's all right, lass, she's going to be all right. It'll be all right, Molly. It's all right!'

For a moment she resisted the words. There was a joy there on the right side of the looking-glass. But there were demons too.

Her father's arms went round her. The undemonstrative, awkward, embarrassed Ivor put his arms round her and drew her close as she could not remember him doing since she was a child. So she stepped back through the glass and wept for the joy of it and the pain of it at the same time.

'She's strong,' said Sterling. 'Very strong. But she's in her sixties, with a hard life behind her. The cancer had checked. It often does, then there's another mighty leap. God knows why.'

'But you got it in time?' said Molly.

He looked at her speculatively.

'You did, didn't you? You said you did!'

'Oh yes,' he said. 'This time. You're an intelligent woman, Mrs Keatley, and I reckon you're strong too. We cut, we don't cure. She'll be all right, I think. But she won't recover in a day. And a few years from now, who knows? But once you've had your three score years and ten, who knows anyway?'

'Are you trying to be pessimistic in an optimistic kind of way, Mr Sterling?' asked Molly.

They were standing in the hospital car park, quite close to the spot where Molly had had her peaceful vision of despair earlier in the day. It was now evening, and though they had been assured by smiling nurses that there was no point to it, she and Ivor had insisted on returning during visiting hours, even if only for a glimpse. Molly had spotted Sterling heading for his car and, sending her father ahead, she had approached him as he was about to drive away. He looked weary, but he had courteously got out of his car and listened to her questions, and either his weariness or his assessment of Molly's strength, was causing him to speak with unusual openness.

'Pessimistic? Oh no. I suspected that before the day was out I would be telling you and your father that Mrs Haddington had a matter of months, or even weeks, to live. And I wasn't being pessimistic then. Well, she *has* got months or weeks to live. But more, many more, I hope, than I expected. So no forecasts. Six months, a year from now, she might be back – almost – to her normal health. Ask me then. I'll probably be as vague. Ten years, fifteen years from now, I might still be being vague! I hope so.'

He got back into his car and started the engine.

Through the open window he said, 'Don't expect much out of her tonight! She'll look awful, hardly be awake.'

'The nurses warned us.'

'Yes, they would. Don't blame them if they seem over-protective. Once you get her home, you'll have to be protective too. She looks the kind of woman who'll expect to be scrubbing the front step in a fortnight! You don't live locally, do you, Mrs Keatley?'

Molly shook her head.

'Well, I'm sure you'll work something out. But she'll need taking care of, and your father won't be able to cope, I shouldn't think. Good night now.'

The ward sister intercepted Molly as she made her way from the lift.

'Your mother's coming along nicely, Mrs Keatley, but she won't be fully awake until tomorrow, you realize that. I don't honestly think there's much point in your father sitting in there.'

'If my mother's asleep, it's hardly going to bother her, is it?'

said Molly sharply.

'No. But it might bother your father,' said the nurse reasonably.

She was right, Molly realized, when she saw her father looking in bewildered pain at the grey haggard face on the pillow.

'She looks worse than she did,' he said incredulously. 'She looked grand yesterday.'

'Oh Dad!' she said. 'She's had an operation. What do you expect? A song and dance act?'

'I don't know. But . . . it's all right, isn't it, Molly?'

He looked at her anxiously as if fearful that he, the working man, had been the victim yet once again of some clever con by the professional classes.

'Yes, really. You remember when Danny had that abscess removed? Remember how dopey he was, lying there all night with the white of his eyes showing and his tongue hanging out.'

Ivor considered the parallel while Molly took her mother's hand and squeezed it gently, saying, 'Hello, Mum. It's me, Molly.'

The eyelids fluttered in what might have been recognition, then closed again.

'Come on, Dad,' said Molly. 'We mustn't disturb her. She'll look fifty times better tomorrow, you'll see.'

On the way home they stopped for a drink once again. After a couple of pints and half a dozen rehearsals of what Sterling had said, Ivor became more cheerful. Above their heads a television set blared inanely as some variety show came to an end. Next followed the news and Molly felt the now familiar constriction of the throat as she anticipated hearing Sam's name. The headlines were uttered sonorously: a close vote in the House; a terrorist attack in Africa; the airport traffic control strike was over; there had been another death in Ireland.

It was a fortnight now, she thought in amazement. (Subjectively it felt like a decade.) But not a public word! What else did these mandarins of Whitehall and the Kremlin manage to keep out of the public eye? But it couldn't last, and mean-

132

while she was doing nothing. No. She thought of the events of the past week and decided nothing was an overstatement. There had been diversions, necessary and unnecessary. There had also been manipulations, restrictions, nudgings, and God knows what depth and breadth of observation.

'I'm just going to the ladies',' she announced.

On her way past the bar, she stopped and changed a note for a handful of ten-pence pieces. There was a telephone kiosk in the main hallway of the pub and a cheerful girl on Directory Enquiries rapidly gave her the number she wanted.

It took half a dozen diallings before she got it unengaged.

'East Midlands Airport. Passenger Enquiries.'

Yes, things were getting back to normal after the strike. And yes, Balkan Tours flight to Bucharest had been rescheduled for 10.30 hours the following morning.

'You've been a long time,' said Ivor. 'I was getting worried.'

'Think I'd been mugged in the lav?' said Molly.

'I got you another of the same. All right?'

'Thanks,' said Molly, sipping her drink. 'Dad, look, this may seem a bit sudden, but I've got to go away. Just for a day or two. I would have said something earlier, but I had to wait till after the operation. And now, well, now that Mum's going to be all right, it can't wait any longer. It's better to go now while she's still pretty well flat out than wait till she's sitting up, if you see what I mean.'

'Sitting up, asking questions. Aye. I see what you mean,' said Ivor. 'It's about Sam, is it?'

'Yes,' said Molly. 'It's about Sam. How did you know?'

'Sticks out a mile,' said Ivor. 'You've not been right since you came.'

'Thanks,' said Molly. She played with her glass, waiting for questions.

When none came she said, 'If anyone asks, just say I've had to go down to London.'

'Depends who it is,' said Ivor.

'What do you mean?'

'Some buggers ask, I'll just tell 'em to mind their own business. Is there owt I can do? I guess there's nowt I can say.'

'You've said enough, Dad,' said Molly. 'Thanks. We'd best

be getting back. Danny'll be wondering what's happened and I'd like to get a bit of sleep. I'll be off at the crack in the morning.'

'The crack' was four a.m. A sleepy Danny looked up, puzzled, from his basket in the kitchen as she quietly unbolted the back door.

Ivor watched her, impassive, with an old raincoat over his blue pyjamas.

'Cheerio, Dad,' she said. 'I'll be back soon as I can. Don't let Mum worry.'

'I won't,' he said. 'And try to keep him, lass. He's a good man.'

All this stealth made her feel absurd. She had no idea whether it was necessary or effective. But if she was going to do it, she might as well do it properly, she thought. So she lugged her overnight bag through the empty streets till she reached a telephone-box where she called a taxi. Thereafter, as she sat in the taxi, then in two trains, then in a second taxi, she looked round her with all the alertness her tired mind could muster and she boarded the plane with as much certainty as was possible that she had not been followed.

All around her were cheerful British holidaymakers, delighted at last to be on their way. She had a window seat close up by the flight deck. Perhaps because of the uncertainties caused by the strike the plane was far from full and she was relieved to discover by the time the engines began to roar for their great orgasmic thrust into the sky that no one had occupied the seats next to her. She couldn't have borne a talkative mum with two excited kids from Bradford.

The noise grew louder, the ground was reluctant to let them go, then suddenly they were unstuck and all those earthbound people and houses and towns became as remote and insubstantial as through the eyes of a man dying.

The warning lights went out. She released her seat-belt and yawned. Perhaps she could sleep. But first she removed her suède jacket to adjust to the well maintained temperature of the cabin. Rising to her feet to place it in the locker above her head, she glanced back down the plane. Most of the passen-

134

gers were peering out of the window trying to glimpse the safe and familiar ground they had so unwisely left. But two pairs of eyes were focused on her. She returned their gaze with the blank stare of a stranger and sank quickly back on to her seat.

Fred Wallace and Sally Ann Hibbert.

So much for my James Bond precautions, she told herself as she looked out of the narrow window.

Below, England had passed from view and the plane seemed to hang motionless above an endless waste of driven snow.

18

Fatigue defeated speculation and Molly rapidly fell asleep only to be awoken twice, the first time by a stewardess trying to give her a plastic meal, the second by Wallace.

'I'm sorry,' he said. 'But we'll be landing soon and I wanted to talk.'

She looked at him groggily, not quite sure where she was. He put his finger on the service button and held it there till a girl detached herself from the duty-free trolley. She did not look pleased, but Wallace was not bothered by looks of displeasure.

'A black coffee,' he ordered. 'And a large Scotch.'

'Where's your friend?' asked Molly. 'Paralytic in the bomb bay, I hope.'

'You're waking up,' said Wallace approvingly. 'Look, first of all, let me say I didn't think you'd be on the plane.'

'You were poking around and saw the ticket,' accused Molly. 'While I was being beaten up.'

'I thought, with your mother . . . How is she, by the way?'

'They think the operation was a success. She should be all right.'

'That's really great,' he said, his face lighting up.

He sounds as if he means it, thought Molly, responding to his pleasure in spite of herself.

'We were going to get an earlier flight, but the strike scuppered that. Then when it was called off, I rang and asked about this flight. There were some vacancies on the package. I didn't think you'd be on it. And if Sam was going to be waiting . . .'

'He'd see li'l ole Sally Ann trip lightly down the steps and they'd fall into each other's arms. And what would you be doing? Running around with a camera and a tape-recorder to the applause of the Rumanian State police?'

The coffee and whisky arrived. Molly sipped the murky brown mixture and shuddered. Wallace uncapped his miniature and shot half of it into her cup.

'Here. That should help,' he said.

It did.

Suddenly Molly laughed.

'What's funny?' said Wallace.

'I'm just thinking of me tiptoeing around like Mata Hari so that I wouldn't be followed to the airport and here you are, probably with half the FBI or whatever in tow.'

'CIA,' said Wallace. 'And no. I've been tiptoeing a lot longer than you. They'll be on the trail sooner or later, but even sooner will be too late.'

'Why?' said Molly. 'What do you think is going to happen?'

'I've no idea. But it shouldn't take long. Time's running short. Sam's masters will only have given him this amount of leeway because it suited their purposes. But they must be ready to unveil him now. Within a week of Llewellyn's performance is how I read it.'

'This plane should have arrived yesterday,' said Molly. 'He may not have waited.'

'In that case, enjoy your holiday,' said Wallace. 'But if he *is* there, I want to see him. Tell him that. Tell him loud and clear so that if there's any of his friends around, they hear too. I don't want anyone imagining I'm one of the cloak-and-dagger boys and greeting me accordingly. Tell him I'll get him a good press, as good as he could look for in the circumstances. It'll help everybody, not least you, Mrs Keatley.'

'If I stay, it won't matter in the least, will it?'

He looked at her steadily.

'That's not how I read you, Mrs Keatley,' he said. 'I'll be sticking close, but in case I lose you, remember – tell him. Good luck.'

He rose and left her. She took another sip of the coffee and suddenly felt very sick. It was lack of breakfast, she assured herself. But her mind took her back to her childhood when the anticipation of any large public occasion – such as acting in the school nativity play or being confirmed – had brought on a fit of vomiting. This was the very nausea of terror.

Identification seemed to bring control and the feeling slowly passed.

'Listen, I just wanted to say I'm sorry.'

How long Sally Ann Hibbert had been leaning over the empty seat, she did not know. She looked up at the smooth-planed face and was pleased to see a slight puffiness and discolouration about the left side of the mouth.

'I was really high. It was stupid. I've never been like that before. High, yes, but not stupid.'

'You were more than stupid,' said Molly. 'You were maniacal.'

'Sorry?'

'You tried to stick a knife in me.'

'Oh Jesus.'

She slid down into the vacant seat and looked at Molly helplessly.

'I did *what*? Freddie never mentioned a knife. Oh Jesus.'

'Freddie was too busy going through my personal possessions to catch the knife-fight. He just turned up in time for the wrestling match.'

Hibbert shook her head in disbelief.

'That makes it different,' she said. 'I wouldn't have bothered you if I'd known. *Sorry*'s all right for common assault, but what do you say for attempted murder?'

'You could try *awfully sorry*,' said Molly.

She hadn't meant to joke, but it came out as a joke. Perhaps it was just that terror dilutes dislike.

The American looked at her with a wry smile.

'Well, I am,' she said. 'Awfully sorry. Look, Mrs Keatley, I don't know what's going to happen down there.'

She pointed to where through broken cloud they could see lying beneath them a picture map in faded pastels of a country whose shapes and forms were very un-English.

'All I know is, I'm scared shitless. I feel like I might just sit on this plane till it turns round and heads back. But I won't. I'll stick around and hope I'll get a turn with Sam. I don't know what deal you've got in mind, but if it doesn't pan out, then I want a go. Is that fair?'

'What deal do *you* have in mind, Miss Hibbert?' asked Molly.

The woman stood up. She looked tired and lost.

'I wish I knew, Mrs Keatley. I wish I knew.'

'Ladies and gentlemen,' announced a voice over the Tannoy. 'In a few moments we will be landing at Otopeni Airport . . .'

They were processed through the airport controls swiftly and efficiently. Molly looked for significant reactions when she presented her passport at the airport and again at the hotel, but observed nothing, though her sense of being observed was very strong. Which was hardly surprising, she told herself. My nerves are tuned to concert pitch. Time to worry when I stop feeling watched!

Her room was on the third floor at the back of the hotel. It had a little balcony overlooking a small garden. Beyond the garden was a car park bathed in sunlight which bounced back off the whitewashed wall of what looked like a warehouse. A gang of small boys were playing football against it and the sight was reassuringly familiar. As she watched, the ball rebounded high into the air and bounced on the roof of a parked car. Its colour was precisely the blue of Sam's Datsun, she thought. But this had a black stripe down the bonnet and was much smaller and of an unfamiliar shape. Its door opened and a large shirt-sleeved man emerged and shouted angrily at the boys, who withdrew with jeers and gestures which grew bolder the farther they got. The man retaliated with an upward flick of his brawny arm, a movement which was at the same time essentially Central European in concept and universal in significance. Then he glanced up at the hotel before getting back into the little blue car which must have felt like an oven.

Molly's bedroom, though the sun was not shining directly on to it, felt stuffy and overwarm too. She had had some faint notion of being contacted as soon as she arrived, or even finding Sam waiting for her at the hotel. Surely there was no need for hide-and-seek here? As far as Sam was concerned, this was a friendly country whose security forces would be only too willing to co-operate if he felt the need.

The courier had announced that there would be a buffet lunch available in the dining-room after they had unpacked. Molly had not eaten anything since the previous night, and then not much. She looked at the bedside phone which lay there, crouched and threatening, as if making ready to ring the moment she left the room.

'Please yourself,' she said and went down to eat.

The buffet consisted mainly of slices of what tasted like peppered spam, hunks of very hard, very dark bread, and segments of large and extremely tasty tomatoes. Sally Ann Hibbert and Wallace were there with a flask of wine on the table between them. They looked up as Molly entered and she felt an impulse to go and join them. But such a union might easily disturb a knowledgeable watcher and extend the period of careful scrutiny which she suspected was now going on. So she sat at a table by herself till joined by an elderly couple who entertained her for twenty minutes with a detailed account of their lives and interesting times, then cordially invited her to take the harp and sing a bit of autobiography.

'I'm rather tired after the flight,' she said. 'Excuse me.'

She lay on her bed until six o'clock, dozing fitfully. Then she rose, showered and went downstairs for dinner at seven. By now things were properly organized and she saw with dismay that her room number was displayed on a table for three at which the elderly couple were already seated and tuning up.

The American woman and Wallace were alone again at the far side of the dining-room.

To hell with it, she thought, and headed for their table.

'May I join you?' she said. 'Don't get ideas. All I want is peace.'

Wallace was as expert with reluctant Rumanian waiters as he was with surly air-hostesses and he rapidly organized a chair and a place-setting for her.

'One question, then no shop,' he said. 'I take it nothing's happened yet?'

'Nothing,' she said.

'Fine. Will you join us in a bottle of plonk?'

He was true to his word and chattered entertainingly about his journalistic adventures abroad throughout the meal. Sally Ann Hibbert ate sparingly and said nothing, but her silence was introspective rather than hostile. Molly found herself thinking that in some ways the American was in a far worse position than she was. What did she imagine – that if Sam couldn't get hold of his wife, he was instantly going to settle for his mistress? Molly wondered how much it was Wallace's pressure that had persuaded her to this move. And, if so, what were his motives?

Dinner over, they retired to the bar. Sally Ann started downing large quantities of very expensive Scotch and, fearful of a repetition of her previous onslaught, Molly excused herself. Wallace nodded slightly, as though approving her decision. She took a turn round the square outside the hotel. It was noisy and full of tourist life. She felt very detached from it all. But she was also beginning to feel angry.

At ten o'clock she went to bed. She had brought her sleeping tablets with her and after tossing and turning for half an hour she got up and, ignoring all the warnings about the water, she washed down a couple of pills. Eventually they worked, and she slept after a fashion, but when she woke next morning she was still fatigued. She lay in bed and regarded the ceiling, thought of her mother opening her eyes to a similarly unstimulating prospect, and gradually found a fatigue-destroying rage building up in her.

'What the hell am I doing here?' she demanded of herself.

Downstairs, she sought out the holiday courier at his breakfast in the staff dining-room.

'I want to fly back to England,' she announced.

He was a brown little man with yellow teeth and she didn't care for them or for the dismissive gesture with which he replied, 'Later, later. No business till after breakfast, please.'

'Yes,' she said. 'By the time I finish *my* breakfast, I expect you to have found out what's the earliest possible flight to get me out of here.'

She headed for the door, paused, and looked around.

He was sitting with his coffee cup in his hand, regarding her uneasily.

'You won't do it by sitting here, swilling coffee, will you?' she bellowed.

Have I always been a bully? she wondered. Or did I merely learn the art from joining a class born to it? If so, I've graduated at last.

The little brown man approached her in the lounge about an hour later, showing his yellow teeth in an ingratiating smile.

'Well?' she said.

'I'm sorry,' he said. 'The earliest is a regular flight at twelve-thirty tomorrow afternoon. There's nothing on one of our charters until Friday. Is it, er, illness? Or a bereavement perhaps?'

'What's it matter?'

'It's a question of expenses. You will have got to pay the fare yourself, you see, but the company takes out an insurance for all its holidaymakers. Illness, bereavement, you can claim for them.'

He seemed genuinely eager to help and Molly softened her attitude to him.

'That's very kind of you. I'll contact the company. How do I go about booking a ticket?'

And will they accept a Barclaycard? she thought in sudden panic. And if they did accept it, would she be able to pay up when the money came due?

'Leave it up to me,' he said. 'All will be arranged.'

He almost backed out of her presence in his new-found delight at giving service. The upper class were right, thought Molly. Shout at foreigners and they get things done.

'All what will be arranged?'

It was Wallace, who had not been at breakfast and who must have come in via the sliding glass door from the little garden while the courier was doing his court exit act.

'A flight out,' said Molly. 'Nothing's happening here. I've got a seriously ill mother and a far from self-sufficient father back home. I can't hang around here all week neglecting them.'

Which was a very noble-sounding motive, she thought. But didn't anger, and fear, and frustration, play a part too? Not to mention sheer boredom. She looked around. The hotel lounge was empty. Everyone else was doing whatever everyone else did on holidays in Bucharest. She couldn't face much more of this emptiness.

'Where's Miss Hibbert?' she asked.

'You're very formal. Still in bed for all I know. No, I mean, I don't know. We're not sharing. It would be undiplomatic in the circumstances, don't you think? When are you going?'

'I can't get a seat till lunch-time tomorrow.'

'Oh?'

He looked thoughtfully at her for a moment.

'Excuse me,' he said.

He went across the lounge and through the arch which led to the reception desk. There he spoke to the receptionist then moved out of sight.

A few minutes later he returned.

'Odd,' he said.

'What?'

'If *I* wanted to get on a flight to England, they could take me at twelve-thirty. Today.'

'What! Why, that stupid little sod!'

All she felt was indignation at this foreign inefficiency. Wallace regarded her quietly.

'Yes,' he said. 'You're probably right. That's all it means. A stupid little sod.'

'What else could it mean?' she asked.

Before he could reply, the receptionist came through the archway.

'Mr Wallace?' she said in tones surprisingly guttural for such a pretty little thing.

'Yes?'

'You are friends with the American lady, Miss Hibbert?'

'Yes. Why? What's the problem?'

'No problem,' smiled the girl. 'A small matter of the passport. But she seems a little bit disturbed. You know, crying a little and some shouting.'

'Oh God,' said Wallace. 'She can't have got drunk already, surely! Where is she?'

'In her room speaking with the manager. Can you come, please?'

'All right,' sighed Wallace. 'See you later.'

Molly watched him cross the lounge with the girl in close attendance. When he reached the lift he hesitated as though something had come into his mind and looked back over his shoulder, as though he thought of retracing his steps. But the receptionist had pressed the button which opened the doors and now she took him firmly by the elbow and urged him in.

143

Two men in dark blue suits strolled in after him, the doors closed, and the lift ascended. The girl did not return to her desk but walked with calm elegance towards the dining-room and disappeared, leaving only the gently swinging double door as evidence that there was anybody in the hotel but Molly.

Even the noise of the traffic outside seemed to have faded to little more than the murmur heard in a sea-shell pressed against the ear.

Slowly Molly stood up and slowly turned.

The sliding door which led into the garden was open. Just outside, framed in sunshine with one foot on the threshold, one in the garden, was Sam.

'Hello, love,' he said.

19

They walked through the garden, he a little ahead of her, glancing round from time to time and smiling encouragingly, like Orpheus leading Eurydice out of the Underworld. Wrong, thought Molly. When Orpheus looked back, he lost his wife for ever. But this is certainly what it must have felt like, this sense of unreality, this movement from the cool shade into the violent glare of the sunlight which bounced back from the white wall on the far side of the car park.

She had not spoken yet. Sam had said 'Let's walk', and she had walked. Nor had they touched though his hand reached back towards her as though her steps were faltering and she might need support. They moved among the cars. The little blue car with the black stripe was no longer there, but the children were still playing with their football. It ran towards Sam who trapped it clumsily, then ballooned it back over their heads with his toe, causing the boys to make wry, disgusted faces at each other.

A large white car was badly parked across the entrance to the car park. An emaciated man in shirt-sleeves leaned against the bonnet but pushed himself upright as they approached. Sam made an impatient gesture and they went by the car, out on to the street.

This silent procession was absurd, decided Molly.

'Where are you taking me?' she asked, very clear, very English.

'Somewhere quiet,' said Sam. 'A coffee. Or a drink.'

He led her along a wide, busy boulevard. It all looked very modern. She had not expected Bucharest to be so modern. After about a hundred yards he paused outside a café on the corner of a quieter narrower street paved with grey stones. The café had a terrace with tables shaded by rather drab rudimentary parasols. It was not crowded, but there were several people scattered around. Smiling, he urged her to enter. A waiter came forward as if expecting them and showed them to an empty table in the coign formed by the square bay of the café window. It was quiet enough, but not as quiet as a hotel room.

'I'm glad you came,' said Sam.

She regarded him helplessly, not knowing what to say. He looked like Sam, yet he did not look like Sam. It was as though an actor had studied the part and been made up as near perfection as is possible.

'What's up?' he said anxiously.

'If you've got a year, I'll tell you,' she said. No, that was the wrong tone. The new, smart, sharp Molly was designed for survival in UK conditions. Out here she needed something different.

'I'm sorry,' she said. 'It's just – I can't believe it's you.'

'What? I've not changed that much, have I?' he laughed. 'It's only a couple of weeks!'

Only! No, he hadn't changed. The round good-natured face, the frank blue eyes, the little scar on the strong jaw showing how his safety-belt had once saved his face from the windscreen but not from the steering-wheel; everything was the same. Except that now for the first time in years she was really looking at him and finding him . . . foreign. That had to be the word!

Suddenly he began ploughing his fingers through his thick grey hair and instantly the new sharp focus went muzzy and he became more like the old familiar Sam.

'What do you want to say to me?' she asked quietly.

'Let's have a drink or something. Coffee for you?'

'No, I'll have a Scotch.'

He raised his eyebrows comically, then summoned the waiter and ordered.

'It costs the earth out here,' he commented. She smiled at that. Sam had never been mean, but he had never thrown money around either. Seeing the smile, he leaned forward as though encouraged and said, 'It's great to see you, Molly.'

She removed her hands from the table in case he should clasp one of them in both of his, a favourite gesture when making some point in a discussion. She wasn't ready for con-

146

tact yet. He observed her withdrawal, frowned, and sat back in his chair.

'What's Wallace doing here?' he asked abruptly.

'He wants to see you,' said Molly. 'He's after a story. He promises you a fair hearing.'

Sam laughed, the familiar bark with which he expressed scornful disbelief. He's making himself real to me by little hints and nudges, thought Molly desperately.

'He always was a chancer,' said Sam. 'He'll be lucky if they don't put him away for a couple of weeks. Traducing the State!'

'And what about Sally Ann?' asked Molly. 'What's to be done with her?'

'Oh,' said Sam. He looked at her guiltily. The waiter brought their drinks, whisky for her and *tuica*, the local plum brandy, for Sam. He must be adept at taking on local colouring, she thought.

'You know about her then? Of course. The bastards would make sure you did! I'm sorry, love. I know it sounds feeble, but I can explain.'

'Hold it, Sam,' she said. 'Get it straight. I'm not here as a jealous wife who needs to be soothed and placated. Ms Hibbert's the least of my worries.'

'Point taken,' he said. 'But listen, anyway. I used to know her years ago. Well, doubtless you got all that history too? They're pretty thorough, I bet. When she turned up again, accidental meeting a couple of months ago, know what I thought?'

'I can guess,' said Molly. 'You can skip the four letter words.'

He shook his head and moved his hands on the table impatiently. She thought, he's dying to grasp one of mine and lift it up almost to his lips, and look me squarely and sincerely in the eyes.

'No, love,' he said. 'You're blaming me for being something I hid from you, right. Well, OK, but it works both ways. You've got to see what I did in the light of what I was hiding.'

'Lift your bushel, you mean?' said Molly.

'I thought they were on to me,' he said quietly, almost to

himself. 'I thought she was a plant. You know, a big double bluff, someone from the US Embassy, openly admitting a link with the CIA! It was so obvious it must be genuine – or was I *supposed* to read it like that?'

'So you went to bed with her!' said Molly incredulously.

'I played along,' he said. 'I didn't know what the game was, so I played it straight.' He laughed without humour. 'You might say I acted naturally.'

She regarded him with horror.

'That's worse than the other!' she protested. 'That's nastier than anything anyone's said about you!'

'Why? Because it makes me sound a cold unfeeling bastard? Never believe it, love. There was a deep, vibrating, ultra-real emotion at the bottom of my relationship with Sally Ann. Fear! All those years, and it never left me. One day, some day, any day . . . strange, you'd think a man'd get used to it. Sometimes I forgot, of course. Nearly all the time with you. But always it came back . . . There you are then! That's my bid for sympathy. How's it grab you?'

This self-mocking coda which traditionally followed his more serious moments was another identity pointer. Much more of this and we'll be exchanging jokey accounts of the last couple of weeks! thought Molly desperately.

'You're telling me it was just a necessary part of your other profession, this bedding of Hibbert? Even though she'd had your child?'

He downed his pale spirit in one quick wristy movement. Now that *was* unfamiliar.

'They *have* been thorough,' he said.

'Oh yes. I've found out a lot,' she said bitterly.

He shrugged helplessly.

'There's a lot I couldn't tell you. Daren't tell you,' he said. 'I'm sorry.'

'Sorry! Sorry you couldn't tell me you were a spy? All right. Perhaps not. It's despicable and it's cheating but perhaps it's understandable. But that you'd had a vasectomy, that you couldn't give me any children, what was there in the KGB fucking rule-book that stopped you telling me that?'

She was shouting and people were looking across at their table with more open interest than they would show in Don-

148

caster. At the entrance to the terrace, the thin shirt-sleeved man was standing looking anxious.

Sam ignored them all. Her hands had come up from her lap to emphasize her anger and now at last he had one of them in his and he was fixing her with that anxious, frank, loving expression.

She did not withdraw her hand but let it rest between his, as cold and unyielding to him as her mind in which she was wishing his departure, his disappearance, his death.

'That too? They told you that? Oh yes, they'd tell you that! Did they tell you that ten years ago, before we got married, before I even proposed but when I knew I was going to, and that you were going to say yes, I went along and had the operation reversed? Did they tell you that?'

She didn't believe him. It was a transparent lie.

'It's not possible,' she asserted. 'It's irreversible.'

'It depends. In some cases, yes. In mine, no. Old Doctor Shaw, he was at the wedding, he fixed it up. He'll still have the records. And the clinic too. They keep a fat dossier on us rich private patients, I bet. Ask when you get back to London. I'll write a letter telling them to reveal all my private parts to you!'

He grinned suddenly and kissed her finger-ends.

'Forget it for now. It's true, but forget it. You can check. You *must* check. But no more now. OK?'

He's telling the truth, she decided. At least, I think he's telling the truth. And he's delighted because this minor victory might divert my main attack!

But for all her attempted cool appraisal, she could not conceal her softening of mood and his hands squeezed hers to acknowledge the relaxation of her muscles. But he made no attempt to hang on when she withdrew it and picked up her drink.

'Another?' he said.

She shook her head.

'I will.' He conveyed his order by a hand signal to the attentive waiter.

'I think I'm going to need it,' he said.

'Why's that?'

'Well, the worst is yet to come, isn't it?'

He smiled at her, his rueful more-sinning-than-sinned-against smile. He was even smarter than she thought. Seeing there was no real chance of his recent victory permanently diverting the main onslaught, he was advancing to meet it on his own ground.

'What do you mean?' she said, refusing to be engaged till she was ready.

'The things they've tried to use to turn you against me, I've been able to sort them out, after a fashion. The vasectomy business, that I can prove. Sally Ann, well, there was an explanation. OK, I know it sounds weak, but it's the truth. The only proof I can offer is that she's here now and I want nothing to do with her. But that still – '

'How did you decide about Hibbert?' she interrupted, still retreating, still postponing the last confrontation.

'Decide what?'

'That she was genuine.'

'That? I never did. I still haven't.'

'*What*? But you rang her to warn her before you went.'

'Why not? Either she was genuine all-for-love, in which case she deserved a warning; or else she – and the tip-off – had been planted; in which case they would know I was running. I thought telling her might make her show her hand, but it didn't.'

'She's been watched then?' It suddenly struck Molly that he'd shown very little curiosity about Hibbert's appearance in Bucharest.

'Distantly. There was too much activity to risk getting close. Even more so with you. That's why there was this palaver with the holiday package. I told them Bucharest was as far as I would go without contacting you.'

'You must be important,' she said, half mocking.

'Not really,' he said. 'It suits the Rumanians to keep me here as long as possible. They're trying not too subtly to pump me! They've been flirting with the Chinese lately and there's not much love lost between Bucharest and Moscow. But they wouldn't risk an open break, so it's useful for them to be able to cite my romantic obduracy as the reason for the delay. I'm just using the situation to get my own way, which is to say, to get this chance to talk to you. Once in Moscow, who knows?

Then I'll be the loyal servant of the State.'

He spoke without much irony and she remembered Llewellyn making his personal statement in Oslo as though he knew he might not have such a chance for free speech again. Yet still he went.

'You tried to ring me,' she said.

'Yes. I got rather drunk and very lonely one night. I almost made it too, but the shutter came down at the last minute. Still, it convinced them I was serious about seeing you.'

'And if I hadn't come?'

'You came,' he evaded. His drink had arrived. He was toying with the glass. She decided that when it was flipped to the back of his throat, the battle would be on.

But not yet. A little while longer. But not in silence, silence was the mother of thought, the enemy of peace.

'I think she is genuine,' said Molly.

'Why?'

'She attacked me. Nearly killed me with a knife.'

Sam was disappointingly unimpressed by this melodramatic news.

'How near was nearly?'

Piqued, she told him about the severed cardigan.

'That would fit both an amateur near miss and an expert near miss,' he answered. 'You say Wallace was there. What was he doing?'

'He was in the living-room. I think he found the travel stuff in the bureau.'

'Ah,' he said. 'Well, there you are!'

'Where?' she asked. 'Where are we?'

They sat in silence for a moment. The table umbrella was fixed so that Molly was in the shade, Sam in the sunshine which touched the ends of his grey hair with a golden halo. The silence stretched on, not to be broken nor to be borne.

'Sam,' she said. 'Molly,' he said.

They had both spoken at the same time. Neither continued.

Then Sam flipped the burning liquor to the back of his throat.

20

'To begin at the beginning,' he said. 'God knows where that is, though! The 'fifties perhaps. Yes . . .'

'No,' said Molly firmly. 'A bit earlier than that, please. I want it all today. No more surprise parties.'

'How much earlier?'

'How about the womb?'

He looked at her in puzzlement, then started to grin.

'I'm with you!' he said. 'No, it's all right. I'm not Ivan Skavinsky Skivar! I'm Samuel Keynes Keatley of Wellington, Salop, all right. Your genuine Shropshire lad!'

It was an old joke between them. She had borrowed the poems to understand it. She had found their studied pessimism morbid and indulgent, but Sam had been a real enthusiast.

'All right,' she said. 'I just wanted to establish whether you were a traitor or merely a spy. Carry on.'

That got the mood right once more. His face set and he spoke now with power and authority and none of the little mannerisms of hesitation and out-loud thinking with which he usually embellished his public utterances.

'It was Hungary that showed me what I believed. I was still at Durham. I wasn't a CP member, but I felt a strong intellectual and emotional commitment to their ideas. After Hungary, all around me I saw fellow travellers and a lot of your actual card-carriers rushing to get off the bus with cries of disgust and outrage. To my surprise, I felt neither. I felt I ought to feel them, but I didn't. So while the rest queued up to resign, I went along to join. That's when it started. I was advised not to take out a formal and public membership.'

'Advised? Who by?' interrupted Molly.

He looked at her with contempt.

'Don't be stupid,' he said.

'You think I'd tell *them*?' she asked, hurt in spite of herself.

'Men have told me more important things for less important reasons than you might imagine you've got,' he answered. 'So I did nothing openly. I'd no idea then that I'd been recruited, you understand. There was a sense of commitment which was deeply satisfying, that was all. I had vague notions of becoming a research scientist, but I wasn't really original enough to do anything important and a year in industry trying to make soap powder wash whiter soon disenchanted me. So I drifted into scientific journalism. You know all this.'

'I've never heard it quite this way before,' said Molly. She felt cool and businesslike, like a magistrate on the bench, recognizing the existence of the human emotional response but willing herself to keep it separate from her judgement.

'That's when they began to sound me out in earnest. I was older now, and wiser. I soon grasped what was going on. So I told them to forget the subtle probing. If there was anything I could do to help the Party, they just had to ask. You should get that quite clear, Molly. I wasn't drafted. I volunteered.'

'Great,' said Molly. 'The bravest and the best always do.'

He looked at her without much expression except for a slight narrowing of the eyes, but that might just have been in reaction to the sun which was now full in his face.

He lifted his hand and signalled to the waiter again.

'Now I see why we're talking here,' said Molly. 'Room service is so much quicker than at the hotel.'

'I wanted to talk privately,' he said.

She looked around and laughed, then she took his meaning and stopped.

'Je-sus!' she said. 'Is it true? And this is what you've run away to!'

'Don't be naïve, Molly,' he said wearily. 'I'd do the same in England. If you've got any sense, so will you. If you go back.'

'What?' she said, suddenly frightened.

Now there was expression on his face and in his voice as he leaned forward and spoke to her low and rapidly.

'This is what you've come all this way to talk about, isn't it? Us. Our future, or our futures, if that's the way you see it? But you don't seem very keen to get to the point, Molly. You keep on ducking away every time we get near. Are you scared? All right, so I'm scared too. But we've got to talk about it. Look, I'm telling you how I got into this, but I see that's not important now. It just developed, like any job does. And at first it was just exciting, knowing something that all around me didn't know. Kid's stuff. Then it became routine for a while. And then the terror started. I reached thirty and that was my birthday present. I suppose it's always a watershed, a time for review. You know what happened on my thirtieth birthday? Labour won the election! The Tories were out after thirteen years. As for CP candidates, they were few and far between and they all lost their deposits. Well, it was a move to the left, a step in the right direction, and I suppose I should have been glad. But I wasn't. I saw as clearly as was possible that nothing would ever change in England. There, gradualism means standing still and revolution means compromise! So I was working for nothing in my lifetime, and that lifetime was going to be spent living a secret, till I was detected, and chased, and perhaps caught and imprisoned – or worse . . .'

'Worse? Come on!' said Molly. 'We don't even hang murderers nowadays!'

He laughed and drank from the latest glass which the waiter had insinuated between them as he spoke.

'No,' he said. 'Not by the thumbs, certainly. I'm sorry, I was getting carried away. Look, all I'm saying is, I began to feel lonely and afraid. And four years later I met you. Do you know, by that time I was beginning to get careless, almost deliberately taking unnecessary risks as though I wanted to get caught! But after I'd met you, I began to be careful again. By God, I began to be so careful. I suppose, in a way, you're responsible for any undermining of the State I may have managed in the last ten years!'

He grinned at her with all the youthful pleasure he'd always displayed in a paradox. She didn't respond. Strangely, she was finding it rather hard to concentrate. It was like talking to a rather boring acquaintance at a party where the line of conversation was hardly worth following through the labyrinth of noise. But here there was no very great noise except for the traffic in the street and the determined chatter of a pair of birds looking for crumbs between the tables.

Sam had always been sensitive to her moods and now he saw that he was losing her, for the grin vanished and his fingers were in his hair again, compulsively ruffling and combing it so that the heavy locks moved in the sunlight like surges in a broken sea.

'I'm sorry,' he said, in a voice so low she could hardly catch the words. 'I wanted you. It was selfish beyond computation. But I deceived myself too. With you, I honestly believed I would never let it happen. Getting caught, I mean. I don't believe in anything hereafter, and if there is, well, I hope we'll be able to laugh at what passes for sins here. No, a lifetime seemed enough, and I thought we could have it. I should have known . . . I suppose I did know, but with you . . . I don't think I ever really let you know how completely and utterly happy I was with you. Every minute of those years. I didn't dare! You'd have thought I was certifiable; or pretending. No, what I was pretending to be was an easygoing, unenergetic, placidly content suburban husband! That was my real secret, Molly. That's how I've really deceived you. I dissembled my love. Like a superstitious peasant, I think I believed that if I advertised my joy, the gods would take it away. Well, I don't have to dissemble any more. OK. So you've found what I am. A spy. A traitor. Find as well that I'm a man who loves you more than perhaps you ever imagined. What I'm going to ask you is monstrous. I want you to stay with me, Molly. I want you to settle down with me to whatever kind of life lies ahead. I was selfish before. When you realized what had happened, you must have thought I was the biggest, most selfish bastard in the universe. Now you see you've only scratched the surface. I want you to give up your friends, your family, your country. All I offer is love. All I promise, from now on, is truth. There. End of message. Over.'

He moved his chair abruptly around the curve of the table so that he joined her in the shade. She continued to stare ahead into the space he had vacated as though a strong afterimage still pressed on her eye.

'What's that signal you make to the waiter?' she asked in a voice which sounded to her as if it came from an ancient phonograph.

He must have beckoned this time, for the waiter came across and Sam spoke to him briefly. Molly took a deep breath and tried to catch her thoughts. She had rehearsed the scene in many ways. In none of them had she expected to be so moved.

'I suppose I should be grateful that you didn't try to convert me,' she said, trying to lighten the mood and play for time.

He didn't reply and when she looked at him he was frowning. At first she thought it was at her attempted levity, but when he spoke she saw that it was directed inwards.

'I'm sorry,' he said, not looking at her. 'I didn't mean to make such a blatantly emotional appeal.'

'You mean, you were faking?'

He shook his head impatiently.

'Of course not. I mean every word of it. But it's not what I want you to base your "yes" or "no" on.'

'Oh, I see,' said Molly. 'It is going to be the dialectic approach after all.'

He smiled wanly. The waiter arrived with her drink. He brought nothing for Sam.

'I'm going now, love,' he said.

She looked at him in alarm. Surely he wasn't going to demand her answer instantly. She had known what that answer would be when she arrived in Bucharest. And she still felt she knew what it was. But now there were acres of talk to traverse before she could honestly feel she had reached that destination.

'We'll talk again,' he said reassuringly, as though sensing her thought. Perversely, the reassurance irritated her.

'Will we?' she said. 'I've got a plane seat booked for lunchtime tomorrow.'

'Yes, I know. Tonight perhaps. I'll get in touch if I can. But otherwise, in the morning.'

'Where? When? I'm fed up with hanging around like a flunkey in an ante-chamber. Let's have a bit of this famous equality.'

He hesitated.

'All right. Here again. Ten-thirty. No, better make it ten.'

'Don't be late,' she said. 'I won't have much time.'

He stood up and said, 'I'm a bit pushed too,' not looking at her.

She followed his gaze. The emaciated man was standing by the white car on the road which ran past the terrace, pointing significantly at his wristwatch.

Molly reached up and put her hand on Sam's arm. It was the first voluntary contact she had made with him, she realized.

'Sam,' she said softly. 'Us apart, are things OK for you? I mean, generally. You know, the future . . . ?'

'There's no way I'd go back, if that's what you mean, love,' he answered. 'Am I sure I've done the right thing? That's a romantic, bourgeois question if ever I heard one! We live circumstantially, Molly, not absolutely. In the circumstances, I've done the only thing. That'll have to suffice.'

Suddenly he bent down and kissed her with untypical fierceness.

'Hold it!' she said. 'You're jumping the gun.'

'Next time we meet, what you may say . . .' He paused, then resumed. 'At this moment, a kiss seemed just possible. In the circumstances, it was the only thing! Take care.'

He walked away. She didn't watch him go.

The rest of the day she spent in a sort of tourist trance, drifting round the town, staring at buildings which seemed to tremble in the burning air, sitting in parks where the grass stretched as fixed and hard as a Glitterwax model. She even bought souvenirs; for her father a gunmetal cigarette-lighter and for her mother a stole of fine lace which she would never wear but which would be all the more valued and admired for its impracticality. She also examined a bright peasant neckerchief which she thought would go well with Trevor's colouring, considered the thought with mingled surprise and horror, but bought it anyway. The trance was turning into a kind of hysterical exhilaration. She moved rapidly from shop to shop, buying things she didn't want, such as postcards, just to have an excuse to talk and laugh with those shopkeepers who had a smattering of English. She tried on hats and cheap jewellery, striking extravagant poses before foxed mirrors, to the applause of eager sellers. She grew hot and thirsty and sat alone at a café table, drinking glass after glass of cold lemon juice till a couple of bold-eyed young men at a neighbouring table tried to engage her in a conversation whose words she did not understand but whose intention required no interpreter. Laughing, she rose and left. They rose too and followed her. She stopped in the middle of the street, turned put her hands on her hips in her best fishwife pose and shouted, 'Why don't you two sod off!'

They too halted, looked abashed, turned and went away, glancing over their shoulders from time to time with a defiance that increased with distance. She watched them out of sight, unmindful of the curiosity she was causing among other passers-by. The thought occurred to her that perhaps the boys had belonged to OGPU or SMERSH or whatever set of initials currently ran the lives of people like Sam, and she found herself laughing once more. Even as she laughed, another part of her mind was wondering if this giddiness (in every sense) meant she was becoming ill, while a third area was regarding sombrely and seriously the problem of her relationship with her husband. Determinedly, she shut this away and concentrated on the giddiness.

Diagnosis was not difficult when she glanced at her watch. It was nearly six o'clock. She had had very little breakfast and nothing since except for whisky and lemon juice, as she roamed around under a burning sun.

It was time to go back to the hotel.

The first person she saw as she entered the foyer was Wallace. He had evidently been watching for her. It must have been a long watch.

'Where the hell have you been?' he demanded roughly.

She felt so washed-out now that all she could do was regard him with a disinterest which was probably more infuriating than anger and say, 'I think that's my business, don't you?'

'Not when it involves me, I don't,' he snapped.

'You invited yourself here,' she said wearily. 'Any involvement is your own choice.'

'Maybe,' he said. 'But I didn't invite a gang of goons from the KGB admiration society to interrogate me and Sally Ann for two hours this morning! You've been with Sam, haven't you? And this was a nice little diversionary tactic to keep me out of the way!'

Molly considered. It made sense.

'Yes, I suppose it must have been,' she said. 'Take it up with your MP. Excuse me.'

She tried to walk by him, but he put his hand on her arm. 'Hold on!' he said.

She swayed slightly as she paused and he looked at her closely, anger fading from his face.

'Are you all right?' he said.

'A bit tired,' she said. 'Do you mind if I go to my room now, please.'

He stood aside and she went into the lift.

It was an act more sybaritic than any she could recall to slide gently into the pleasantly warm water that filled the huge old-fashioned bath which must have been constructed with Rumanian giants or small family parties in mind. For ten minutes or more, she just lay there and enjoyed a sense of elemental unity, as though the scented water and the steamy air and her own soft pink flesh had no separate existence, and her mind was just sufficiently aware to apprehend her pleasure. But physical well-being, unlike physical discomfort, had no arts to direct her mind for long, and slowly, inexorably, thoughts of Sam began to rise.

She had told him nothing of her mother, she realized. He couldn't have known, or else he would have mentioned it. But he had known she was staying in Doncaster. Well, that wouldn't have been difficult to deduce, and in any case he had made it clear that a long-distance watch was being kept on her. If it was so distant that nothing had been passed on about her mother, presumably the business with Trevor had gone unremarked also. What if he *had* known? she asked herself defiantly. Her justification for giving herself to Trevor was at least as strong as his for the affair with Hibbert. But she was glad it hadn't come up. It would have complicated matters.

The same applied to her mother's illness, she decided. There was no question but that she had to go back to England. No plea of Sam's, no response of her own, could alter that. But to have mentioned it today would have seemed to imply a conditional acceptance of his offer and she had no desire for misunderstandings. Any future with Sam could only have one basis: complete and continual frankness. Their married life had been built around a deception so great that only an equal openness could make viable its future.

And even then . . . what was it that Sam was offering? A life of exile. Compensation? This passionate, undying love which he claimed to feel – to have always felt – for her. She had been moved. She had responded to it. There was no denying that.

On the other hand, consider the implications. The Sam she had married and loved, this had been a steady, humorous, reasonable, mature, reliable, perhaps even forecastable, above all comfortable Sam. All the things which gauche, eager, touchy Trevor hadn't been. Well, she'd been wrong about Sam. She'd been wrong about Trevor too, or at least time had changed what she in her own youthful arrogance had labelled as immutable. Now Sam was asking her to approve another change, one which involved a leap in the dark which made Trevor's maturation seem like the first faltering steps of a child.

Could she trust Sam? Hardly! On his past record, not at all. Yet, want her he must, else why all this fiddle? But the bigger question was, even if she believed him, did *she* really want this new model? He was offering her passion, excitement – at least she assumed he was. Whereas what a woman considering abandoning home, friends, family and country to live among foreigners in a waste of snows wanted was reassurance! Passion, excitement – that was what won tricks in dull old Donny. Security in the snowdrifts, sex in the slag-heaps, that was the formula for a bearable life.

For that, she thought sadly, was the most she could hope for, perhaps the most she deserved, from this wreck – a life that was bearable. And it seemed at this moment far from certain.

Abruptly she pulled out the plug, stood upright and switched on the shower attachment over the bath as the water gurgled between her legs. The cold spray took her breath away and for a second brought utter freedom from thought.

When she'd had enough she turned it off and stepped out of the bath.

In the silence that followed the cessation of the shower, she heard her bedroom door open.

'Sam?' she called. 'Sam!'

Grabbing a towel, she went out of the bathroom.

'Sam,' she said again, certain that he had come as he said he might.

But the figure sitting on the bed, smoking a cigarette and regarding her quizzically was Sally Ann Hibbert.

21

'What the hell are you doing here?' Molly snapped.

The American laughed.

'Just dropped in for a bit of girl-talk,' she said. 'Were you expecting someone else?'

'Only my husband,' retorted Molly angrily.

'Is that so? You were going to make him an offer he couldn't refuse?'

She let her eyes run slowly up and down Molly's body. With an effort of will Molly prevented herself from wrapping her towel protectively around her torso.

'Have a good look,' she said. 'We're all entitled to a bit of nostalgia.'

'It's not the styling, it's the motor that matters, honey,' said Sally Ann. 'Sam always reckoned you were missing on a couple of cylinders, you know that?'

'I wouldn't place much reliance on anything Sam said to *you*, Miss Hibbert,' said Molly, as coldly as she could. 'You were a piece of insurance, that's all. If you'll excuse the phrase, he was taking you for a ride.'

'That's what he told you, huh?'

The American sighed wearily and looked for somewhere to stub her cigarette. The sag of her shoulders put ten years on her and Molly's anger faded as quickly as the other woman's aggression.

'Here,' she said, picking up an ash-tray from the dressing-table and dropping it on the bed.

'Thanks. Hey, listen, Sam never said that about you. I was just trying to needle some info out of you. I wish now I'd tried kindness.'

Molly began to towel herself vigorously. The American lit another cigarette.

'That was your cue to say, "Me too. I was angry. I made it

162

up." No matter. I wouldn't believe you. What else did he say? About me, I mean. The rest is your business. Not that I wouldn't like to know, being naturally nosey. But anything he said about me, I figure I'm entitled.'

'I don't know if I'm entitled to tell you, though,' said Molly slowly as she slipped on her underclothes. It was a relief to be covered up, not just for modesty's sake either. She still remembered Hibbert's assault on her – could it be only three nights ago?

'Here,' said the American. 'Smell my breath. I've kept off the stuff all day, even after those guys tore my nerves to shreds with their stupid questions this morning. That was one of Sam's tricks, I bet. So anyway, I've been keeping dry just in case I got a chance to talk to him. My guess is it's not worth it. Sober or drunk, I'm off his list. Am I right?'

'He's not going to tell me anything different, is he?' protested Molly.

Sally Ann Hibbert regarded her with a crooked smile.

'You're a nice kind of girl, you know that?' she said. 'Or perhaps you've just decided you're not going to believe anything the bastard tells you ever again. What the hell, if once we stop being suckers, what's left?'

She stood up and smoothed her hair in front of the dressing-table mirror.

'You've a pretty fair body,' she said. 'But don't think I'm giving up. I had his kid, did you know that?'

'Yes, I knew that,' said Molly.

'That should count for something, don't you think? But there's more. I told him the kid was born dead. She wasn't. I signed adoption papers, hardly even saw her. But she was alive, still is, I guess. Almost twenty.'

Molly was pulling a dress over her head so she could not see Hibbert's face. Nor did she want to at that moment.

'Why are you telling me this?' she asked through the printed cotton.

'I may be wrong, but I'd bet on you feeling obliged to pass it on. Then we may get to talk. After that, who knows?'

Molly's head emerged. She smoothed the dress down and sat at the dressing-table to brush her hair.

'Who knows?' she echoed. 'We're not too late for dinner, I

hope. I'm starved. I haven't had a thing since breakfast.'

'I'll tell them you're on your way,' said the American. 'You need the food. Your ribs are beginning to show.'

Molly lingered longer than she had intended over her make-up in her determination to conceal any signs of fatigue or tension that might show. Perhaps Sally Ann *was* working for the CIA and all her emotional involvement with Sam was a pretence, but Molly could not really believe it. Anyway, it made no difference. Agent or inamorata, the woman was a sexual rival and you didn't let the opposition know when you were feeling weak.

But as she slipped into her seat at the dining table, she had the feeling that the American's sharp and still sober eyes were assessing every line and grain of her make-up.

'We waited for you,' said Wallace.

'Thanks.'

They ate in silence, partly through choice, partly because the waiters seemed bent on bringing their tardy table up to the same level of progress as those which had started half an hour earlier. Molly's appetite had not been illusory. She washed the food down with frequent draughts of the soft red wine with which the journalist kept her glass well supplied. She wondered if he had hopes of getting her drunk so that she would reveal details of her encounter with Sam, or the time and place of the next meeting. If so, he was about to be disappointed. It would take a great deal more than half a dozen glasses of wine during the course of a heavy meal to breach the dyke of her discretion, though the surfacing of such a strange metaphor was in itself a warning to take note of.

'No more wine,' she said as the bottle came her way again. 'But I'll have some of their terrible coffee.'

'What about some of their awful plum brandy?' said Wallace.

She shook her head, smiling.

'Look,' said Wallace. 'Can we talk about it? You saw Sam today. OK, so most of what you discussed must have been private, intimate, personal. My bet is he wants you to stay with him, start a new life in Moscow or wherever he ends up. And the Russkis, now they've thought about it, won't be averse to having you quietly in the background when they do the big unveiling ceremony. They're a sentimental lot, really. The family that spies together, sties together. Old Cockney Russian proverb. Well, that's your decision. Either way it doesn't affect my interest in Sam. So tell me, was I mentioned? Did you give him my message? What did he say?'

'Yes. Yes. He described you as a "chancer", said you would be lucky if they didn't lock you up for traducing the State. End of message,' said Molly.

To her surprise Wallace didn't look too put out.

'It's a start,' he said. 'At least the idea's in his mind.'

'It sounded pretty final to me,' said Molly.

'You're forgetting,' said Wallace. 'Sam is no longer a free agent, in any sense of the phrase. There's no way he can decide voluntarily and independently to give an interview to a lackey of the capitalist press. Look, when are you seeing him again?'

Was he *really* trying to trick the information out of her? wondered Molly. It was a bit blatant to be called subterfuge!

'I don't know if I am,' she said.

'Oh, come on!'

'I've got a seat on a plane leaving at twelve-thirty tomorrow, remember? I'm going to be on it.'

He exchanged glances with Hibbert.

'Of course,' he said. 'Your mother. You'd have to go back anyway. Sam would understand that. But he'd want a decision in principle. Would I be right in saying that you've agreed in principle to join your husband as soon as the situation at home permits?'

He had suddenly become the interviewer rather than the dinner-table conversationalist.

'No,' she said in alarm. 'You write anything like that and I'll sue you. In fact, you write anything about me and I'll sue you!'

He was unperturbed by the threat.

'So. No agreement in principle. You know, I don't think Sam's going to let you go till either he's got that agreement or he's had such a definite *No* that he believes it. Which means he's going to see you again whether you've planned it or not. I wouldn't bank on that plane seat being available if I were you.'

Sally Ann Hibbert came into the conversation for the first

time since the meal began.

'For Christ's sake, Freddie, leave the girl alone. She's got problems enough without having a smart-alec reporter on her back.'

What's this? wondered Molly. The tough guy/nice guy interrogation routine?

'Don't be so holy,' sneered Wallace. 'You want to see Sam, who's your best hope, me or Mrs Keatley here?'

The American looked at Molly calmly, at Wallace contemptuously.

'With hopes like these, who needs despair?' she said. 'I'm for the bar. This cold turkey's giving me goose pimples.'

She rose and strode purposefully towards the door.

'Mrs Keatley, Molly,' said Wallace, 'I'm sorry if . . .'

'I know,' said Molly wearily. 'You're only doing your job. Excuse me.'

She overtook the American at the reception desk.

'This is nice, honey,' she said. 'You've come to save me from the demon drink?'

'You mistake me,' answered Molly coldly. 'A messenger, yes. A nurse, no way. The bar's that way, isn't it?'

Frowning, Hibbert withdrew. Molly, after several minutes' negotiation with a new receptionist whose English was broken beyond repair, managed to get through on the telephone to the airport booking office where a man with an Oxford accent assured her that she had a seat on the twelve-thirty flight to London the following day.

Relieved, she replaced the phone. Wallace was just coming out of the dining-room. He spotted her and began to approach but, ignoring him, she made for the lift.

In her room, she locked the door. If Sam intended making a personal appearance tonight, he'd just have to knock. She sat waiting for two hours. The future stretched puzzlingly before her, but to her surprise all she could think about was whether, if he did come now, he would want to spend the night with her. And if he did, would she let him? And if she did, how would she find this new creation whose volcanic passion for her had had to be banked down all these years? The idea made her smile and in the end about eleven o'clock she took a couple of sleeping tablets and went to bed.

This would really test his volcanic passion, she thought sleepily. If he came now, knocking would not be enough. He'd have to break the door down.

22

In the morning, the door was still intact.

So much for volcanic passion, she thought sleepily.

Despite the tablets, she had woken early and though this was not planned, she saw now how she could take advantage of it. After a quick cold shower to get herself fully awake, she packed swiftly and efficiently. When she had finished she looked at her watch. Barely half past seven. Wallace and Hibbert were going to make a determined effort to keep her in their sights this morning, she felt sure. Doubtless Sam had arranged for them to be taken care of again, but it was equally probable that Wallace would have prepared evasionary tactics this time. Well, they could battle it out any way they wanted. She would be out of sight till the hour of her appointment.

A tatty do-not-disturb sign hung behind the door. She went out into the corridor as quietly as possible and hung the sign on the outside. Then, closing the door gently, she made for the stairs.

She was not the first up by any means. Children on holiday can hardly wait for the day to begin. But no one paid her any particular attention as she left the hotel by the garden door and strolled casually away with the air (she hoped) of someone taking a healthy preprandial stroll.

Once out of sight of the hotel, she increased speed and started putting a couple of miles between herself and the hotel, with frequent changes of direction and sudden glances over her shoulder to check on and counter possible pursuit. In the end, recalling Wallace's antics at the racecourse in Doncaster, she was overcome by a strong sense of the ridiculous, and settled down to a steady stroll.

By half past eight she was feeling quite peckish and equally lost. The sight of an open-air museum that she had visited on her crazy tourist trip the previous afternoon gave her her bearings and she walked on till she found a small, rather scruffy café which was open. Its clientele seemed to be mainly workmen enjoying (she guessed) the first break in a day which had started about six. They looked at her with curiosity ranging from the neutral to the sexual, but she felt too wrought up to be intimidated. The Rumanian word for coffee she had picked up and a simple mime and a spot of firm English pointing produced a couple of wheat-bread rolls and a chunk of the spicy spam she had encountered at the first hotel meal. Her lack of self-consciousness must have communicated itself to the other customers for they soon went back to their own conversations and concerns.

She enjoyed the coffee so much that she had another cup. It was not that it was particularly good coffee, she decided. But it was good *something* and five times better and four times cheaper than the stuff in the hotel.

It was a quarter past nine when she left the café. The morning sunshine was perfect, warm without burning, and touching everything, near or distant, with a limpid clarity that magnified without distorting. Instead of the feverish urgency of her perambulations the previous day, there was a growing sense of peace and contentment as she strolled through the streets. Her tensions seemed to be smoothed away by the balmy air and her fears vaporized and drew gently upward by the warming sun. She recalled the recognition of despair she had experienced outside the hospital on the day of her mother's operation. This feeling was not unlike it, except that *then* she had been able to imagine no good and *now*, whatever the evidence of her reason, she could anticipate no evil.

It wasn't that she had reached any decision. As she took her seat at the corner table on the café terrace a few minutes before ten o'clock, she was no more aware of what she intended to say to Sam than she had been when she woke up. But the right words would come, she was certain of that. She remained in this blissful state until the hands of her watch reached ten-thirty. At ten forty-five she began to feel anxious. Perhaps he had sent a message to the hotel changing the plan, and her stupid cleverness in getting out so early had prevented its delivery. But by eleven she had reasoned that, knowing the message had not been received and knowing that

169

she would be keeping the rendezvous at ten, it would have been the easiest thing in the world to get in touch with her here.

Now her mood began to change from anxiety to anger. Perhaps behind all this was the simple arrogant assumption that she would miss her flight rather than abandon the appointment. A kind of test even! No, that was too preposterous; something had happened, but not something that Sam felt it necessary to communicate to her; the assumption was there, she felt it; the assumption that she would wait; at most, go back to the hotel and wait there. He was partly right, she told herself in a cold fury. She would go back to the hotel, but just to grab her case and jump in a taxi. Otopeni airport was several kilometres outside the town and even now she was going to be pushed for time if the traffic were bad. But anything was better than sitting obediently here waiting for master to whistle her to Moscow.

She stood up. She did not offer to pay her bill nor did the hovering waiter seem to expect it. As she left the terrace a big white car came speeding along the busy main road and turned into the quiet side street which ran alongside the café, linking the main road and a tree-lined avenue running parallel to it. The car looked familiar and Molly paused at the corner to watch as it screeched to a halt at a vacant parking space half way down the side street. The back door opened almost before the car had stopped and Sam stepped out. He had seen her for he waved and, looking with his customary care to left and right, he crossed the street and started walking along the pavement towards her. This was the sunny side of the street and she could see every detail of his face, almost every pore, and his fingers were harrowing his hair. Her anger disappeared as it nearly always had at the sight of him. She had to get to the airport, on that she was adamant. But they could go together and talk on the way. She would not tell him yes, but she would not tell him no either. This was no way to settle things between them, here in a couple of hasty meetings in this unfamiliar city. They needed time together, completely together. Let him go to Moscow, let the dust settle, then perhaps with her mother recovered she could join him and for a week, or two weeks, longer if necessary, pick over the wreck of their lives together and see whether or not it was worth the salvaging.

She started to walk towards him. He was only about thirty feet away when suddenly he stopped. His expression changed. Apprehension; annoyance; indignation. Molly looked over her shoulder.

Behind her at the corner of the street were Wallace and Sally Ann Hibbert.

'Go away!' Molly screamed.

Wallace ignored her and advanced determinedly.

'Sam,' he called. 'Just a couple of minutes. OK?'

Hibbert said nothing but came forward too, though with much less certainty.

And now time changes and becomes eternally present.

Sam looks at Molly with a wry smile.

She smiles back.

She is glad that Sally Ann has turned up as well as the reporter. Sam must know that she certainly wouldn't bring the American here.

Now Sam turns and begins to run diagonally across the street to his waiting vehicle. The line of shadow almost bisects the street, turning its grey stoned surface into two equal blocks of black and silver. Sam is crossing from silver to black. From the avenue a car appears. It is bright blue. Sunlight scintillates off the windscreen and the polished bodywork. It is moving very fast and skids almost into the sunlit kerb with a thin wail of stretched rubber. Recovering without loss of speed, it moves back towards the knife-edge of shade, catches it, holds it, runs along it to where Sam stands poised like a wire-walker. He is flicked into the air like a monkey on a stick. Up and over he goes. On and out of sight goes the blue car, forcing its way into the busy boulevard amid a protest of horns.

And Sam lies twisted and still across the line of darkness with a trickle of blood running from his head, scarlet in the shade but already dulling to brown as it touches the sunbaked stone beyond the shadows.

23

Ages passed. In them Molly was transfixed in air by shafts of sunlight with a scream as long as the Milky Way stretching from her twisted mouth as the blue car came round the corner again and again.

Others were passing the time less painfully. She saw Wallace taking photographs of the body till the men from the white car seized his arms and wrenched his camera from him. She saw Sally Ann Hibbert kneel by the body and lift up a lifeless hand in a grip which might have been a lover's farewell or an effort to take a pulse. She saw waiters and customers come out of the café to view the body; she saw pedestrians rush by from the boulevard to get close to the body; and soon the street was so full of people that the body was completely hidden from her sight.

Yet all the time she saw the blue car come round and round the corner.

Someone was grasping her arm tightly.

'Mrs Keatley! Mrs Keatley!' a voice said urgently in her ear. She took no notice till the grip on her arm tightened and she felt herself being dragged backwards through the crowd. She turned to look at her assailant, as indifferent to his identity and purposes as she was to that empty husk, nothing to do with Sam, lying lost for ever in the forest of feet.

It was Aspinall, his face twisted with concern, his wave of golden hair as smooth and perfect as sculpture.

'There's nothing to do, Mrs Keatley. Please come. Believe me, it's best that you come,' he urged as he hurried her along the side street to the main thoroughfare.

She had no power of resistance, nor indeed any thought to resist. I am in thrall, she thought, and wondered why such a curiously archaic phrase should have come to her mind. There was no road she would not have let herself be led along at this moment. Thus indifferently must those queues of defeated Jews have shuffled along towards the camps that would kill them.

A car was waiting, neither white nor blue, but a dusty grey. Aspinall pushed her into the back seat and the car was moving before he himself had wholly entered and closed the door.

'We're going to the airport,' he said, looking at his watch. 'Believe me, it's for the best. There's all kinds of trouble here, Mrs Keatley. Your presence can only complicate things, to say nothing of the pain for you. Believe me, it's for the best.'

They reached the airport with barely twenty minutes to spare. Aspinall was met by a man who handed him an envelope which appeared to contain all her necessary documents.

'Please hurry,' he urged.

She hurried.

'Don't worry about luggage, it'll follow,' he panted as they half walked, half trotted across the concourse. He sounded in very poor condition, she thought. Or perhaps he was asthmatic. He certainly gave the impression of being pretty athletic when he was standing still. But appearances could deceive.

The other passengers were already aboard the plane. No one paid them any attention except for the odd accusing stare as though they had delayed the plane's departure. But in fact it was twelve-thirty precisely as the engines began to shudder and howl in that final frenzy which was to hurl the great machine into the sky.

Molly looked out of the window. The ground fell away. She watched for as long as she could see the foreign fields beneath, but in the end their faded pastel colours disappeared completely as a light mist intervened.

Then she spoke to Aspinall for the first time.

'You killed him, didn't you? That car was waiting in the hotel car park the day I arrived. You let me go loose in England, hoping that I would lead you to where he was before the Russians had put him on show. And I did. And you saw your chance. And you killed him.'

And when she had said that she turned away from the blond man and did not speak to him again, or listen to him, until the plane landed at Heathrow.

Monk met them at the airport. He said nothing immediately to Molly but talked in a low voice to Aspinall while she stood to one side with the obedient patience of a milkman's horse.

'This way, missus,' he said finally.

When they got outside, another car was waiting. This was what transport should be like, thought Molly, everything ready to move off as soon as she stepped into it. It had been a good day for transport.

'Your mam's doing well,' said Monk.

There was something odd about him, she thought.

'What?'

'Still a bit weak, but bossing the nurses. And your dad's managing. They wanted to put the snooker final off. It's to-night. But he said no, he'd play as long as they could start a bit later to fit in with visiting hours.'

He wasn't wearing his cardigan, she realized. Instead he had a brown checked waistcoat, old and stained, it was true, but on Monk the effect was almost rakish.

'You know everything, don't you, Mr Monk?' she said. 'Know everything, fix everything. Life won't surprise you much.'

'Sometimes,' he said. 'Aspinall says you've got hold of some daft idea about us being responsible for what happened over there.'

'Oh no,' she said. 'How could I? The car that killed my husband just happened to be hanging around the hotel car park the day I arrived. Aspinall just happened to be strolling past the road end when the accident happened. I just happen to have been whisked back to England in ten minutes flat.'

'This car,' said Monk. 'In the car park. What kind was it?'

'I don't know the make. What's it matter? Pretty small, blue, with a black stripe on the bonnet.'

'And the car in the accident?'

'I've told you!' she said, at last beginning to get angry. Why haven't I been angry up till now? she wondered. There was a lot to be said for getting angry. 'It was the same. Who else would want him dead but your lot?'

'The Rumanians perhaps, as a favour to Peking. Or the

CIA, led there by Hibbert. Or perhaps even the Russians, thinking he's been bought by Bucharest,' Monk answered with the slightly irritated patience of a man who could extend his list for ever. 'This car was blue, you say?'

'Yes!'

'And the one that hit your husband. You're sure it had a black stripe?'

She thought hard. The blue car came round the corner. Again. And again. And again.

She began to cry.

'It doesn't matter,' she sobbed. 'I don't know about the black stripe. But it doesn't matter.'

She leaned back in her seat and closed her eyes partly in an effort to stop the tears, partly as a signal that she wanted to talk no more. When the tears stopped she dozed fitfully, waking and feeling surprised as the car slowed or accelerated, then falling back into the welcome greyness, till at last there came a dream of Sam so vivid that she woke completely in a moment and found herself slumped across the seat with her head on Monk's shoulder.

She sat upright and looked out of the window.

'This is Eastern Avenue, isn't it?'

'That's right,' said Monk.

'Where're we going?'

'Where would you like to go?'

She thought a moment.

'I'd like to go home, sort out some stuff there, get everything straight, then go up to Doncaster.'

'That's what I reckoned,' said Monk.

She looked at him curiously. He wasn't even smug. Perhaps you didn't need to be if you were always right. Briefly she considered his denial of complicity in Sam's death. There were three possibilities. It had been an accident. It had been murder and Monk knew nothing about it. It had been murder and Monk had arranged it.

She found herself surprisingly uninterested in which of the three held the truth. Perhaps her attitude would change, but certainly she had moved from the state of shock which had enveloped her during the journey home into a state which felt more normal, or at least more rational.

Just how fragile this state was she realized when she opened her front door and found on the hall floor a stack of letters, mainly addressed to Sam. This was just the start. The whole house was full of his presence. She had not realized how much her retreat to Doncaster had put her beyond the range of this constant bombardment of memories.

Her first instinct was to pass swiftly through, grabbing what she required for a long-term absence and heading north that same day.

She said nothing of this but wandered aimlessly around the house for a while, finally returning to the lounge where Monk was standing in front of the fireplace.

'My advice is, get it sorted, missus,' he said. 'Do a job of clearing up here so next time you come there's not so much to bother you.'

'I didn't ask for your advice,' she said.

But he was right again.

He was also extremely useful.

Once he saw that she was going along with his suggestion he did most of the work, sorting out the bills and official correspondence, making out cheques for her to sign and drafting letters for her to type. Midway through the evening she thought of food.

'I could open a tin of soup,' she said.

'Too posh round here for a chippie, missus?'

'It's about a mile away,' she said.

'Grand,' he said. 'I'll have a haddock if they've got one.'

'It'll be cold by the time I get back,' she protested.

'Not if you drive.'

She looked at him, puzzled. His car and driver had disappeared as soon as they had disembarked.

He dipped his hand into his jacket pocket and produced a set of car keys.

'That Jap thing of yours is back in the garage,' he said without looking at her. 'They've put it back together again, I hope.'

She took the keys and went out to the garage. The car was there. It had been washed and polished so that the scratch left by the rose-bush was barely visible.

She got in and had to adjust the seat. Well, even Monk couldn't think of everything.

After their fish and chips, they sat in the kitchen and drank Nescafé laced with Scotch.

'Why are you doing all this, Mr Monk?' asked Molly abruptly. 'Guilt?'

He sipped his coffee noisily.

'Sentiment,' he said.

She laughed, more naturally than she would have thought possible a few hours earlier. Examining her feelings now, afraid of finding she had grown cold and hard, she discovered to her surprise that the theory of vacational relativity she had once worked out with Sam applied even here. It stated that not only did holiday time pass more quickly than real time, it also receded more quickly. And foreign holidays receded most quickly of all. She had seen her husband killed in a Rumanian street that same morning. Yet now she found herself regarding the event with something of the same incredulity with which one might say, 'To think, only a few hours ago I was looking at the Parthenon, walking down Fifth Avenue, swimming in the Dead Sea . . .!'

No doubt there would be a shock of recognition when the snapshots were developed for the holiday album.

'Are you staying the night?' she said.

'I'll be right down here,' said Monk. 'I don't sleep much, missus.'

'Please yourself, but the house is full of bedrooms. I think I'll turn in now.'

She went upstairs. Two minutes later she was down again.

'You've taken all Sam's stuff out of my bedroom,' she said. 'What the hell right do you have to go poking around up there?'

'I put it in the box room while you went out for the chips,' said Monk. 'Shall I fetch it back?'

'No,' she said. Anger didn't touch this man. He was like an s.f. star ship, surrounded by force shields which absorbed all emotional attack. Sam had had something of the same quality, only in his case it had come across as placidity. Monk was as placid as a tiger waiting by a water-hole.

She turned and went back upstairs.

'Just yell if there's anything else you want,' he called after her.

Was that a sexual innuendo? Hitherto she had regarded Monk as being as asexual as his name. Nothing had happened to alter that, had it? She snibbed her bedroom door, but after a few seconds in bed got up and unsnibbed it. Not because she had the slightest desire that he should come, but if he did she did not wish him to think that she had feared the attempt, which convoluted reasoning continued the occupational therapy of the day's work and permitted her to fall asleep almost immediately.

In the morning the holiday snapshots came.

She woke, yawned, stretched. And remembered.

She wept uncontrollably and saw no reason why she should not lie there weeping all day or all the rest of her life if need be. But the sound of footsteps on the stairs, pausing on the landing outside her door, made her muffle her sobs against the pillow and she gained enough strength from that small acknowledgement of an outside world to get out of bed when the steps receded. Speed was of the essence, she realized instinctively. So she washed and dressed with haste and did not even permit the sound of voices from below to make her hesitate on the stairs.

In the kitchen she found Monk talking with Iain Haddon.

'Molly, I'm that sorry,' he said to her as he put his arms about her. He smelt and felt exactly as a Scot should, tweedy, prickly, and Christmassy – a mixture of plum-pudding, pipe tobacco and strong spirit. Over his shoulder she saw the whisky bottle on the draining-board.

'Are you all right?' he asked, looking anxiously into her face.

'Fine, Iain,' she said briskly, disengaging herself. 'Did Mr Monk summon you? He's good at summoning people.'

Haddon looked startled and hurt.

'No,' he denied. 'They got in touch with me from the office as soon as the news came in over the wire. I rang at once just

on the off-chance you were here and Mr Monk answered, so
naturally I...'

'Over the wire?' Molly interrupted in alarm. 'What do you
mean?'

Haddon glanced at Monk, who picked up one of a pile of
papers on the kitchen table and handed it to her without comment.

It was just a small item. *British Journalist in Hit and Run
Accident*. Sam, it said, had been visiting friends in Bucharest
after covering a scientific convention. He left a wife but no
children. In one of the papers there was a blurred picture
that could have been anyone.

Molly stared in disbelief. She had not even considered this
possibility. She'd somehow assumed that Sam would now just
disappear, his body removed in an unmarked van, his presence
in Rumania wiped away as completely and easily as his blood
from the polished grey stones.

'Why didn't you warn me?' she demanded. 'I could have
rung Dad last night. Now he'll see this. And Mum too. You
bastard!'

She was making for the phone when he took her by the
arm.

'It's taken care of, missus,' he said. 'I sent Aspinall up to see
your dad first thing. He said he was from the Foreign Office
and told him that you were all right and would be coming
home today. Your dad took it well, better than from you, I'd
guess.'

'Thank you,' said Molly. 'That was very thoughtful.'

Monk nodded. She realized that she trusted his concern
much more than Haddon's.

'What about my mother?'

'They'll keep it from her for a day or two. But she'll have
to be told. Once she starts having visitors again, there'll be
no way for her not to know. But she'll bear up. She'll have
you and her man to pull her through. She'll bear it better
than a scandal, missus. It's a class thing. The aristocracy's
grand at riding scandals, but ordinary working people are best
when it comes to tragedies.'

This amazing piece of sociology left Molly silent. Haddon
took her hand.

'My dear,' he said. 'It's a terrible thing that's happened. Terrible. But you'll have to weigh it against what's been avoided. I don't know how deep Sam was into this other business, but one thing's been made clear to me, he was away for ever. You'd have had an awful choice to make, Molly. It could have torn you in two. This way, what you've got is honest pain and a healing wound.'

She looked at him and remembered that he had given Wallace her parents' address.

'Iain,' she said wearily, 'why don't you piss off?'

The thought of Wallace put something else into her mind. To Monk she said, 'Do you think you can keep it quiet? What about Wallace and that American woman?'

'They're being held,' said Monk with satisfaction. 'The Russians don't think it was an accident either. Them two were a bit too handy. By the time they get back here, there'll be nothing to print. Her own people'll wrap Miss Hibbert up and no editor will listen to Wallace. No proof, no pictures, no story. That's the way of journalism, isn't it, Mr Haddon?'

'There'll be a bit more arm-twisting than that,' said Haddon cynically. 'As I know.'

'So, that's that,' said Molly. She looked at the kitchen clock. It had been in here on just such a morning of uncertain sunshine only three weeks ago that she had been drying the breakfast dishes and heard Sam return unexpectedly.

Sam.

'What will happen to him? His . . . the body, I mean.'

'They'll send it back,' said Monk.

That hit harder than anything yet. It was obvious, but she hadn't thought it through. There would be a funeral; black umbrellas, dripping yews, muted voices, pious platitudes; then the interested audience of old friends watching the new creature emerge from its crape chrysalis and deciding whether it was admissible or not.

Something of horror, mistaken perhaps for grief, must have appeared on her face for she realized that both Monk and Haddon were regarding her with sympathetic concern. She wasn't having that. Her grief and her horror were her own. She would nurture and shape them in her own way in her own time.

Haddon said, 'Molly, if there's anything I can do. Perhaps a wee stay with Jean and me . . .'

'No, thank you, Iain,' she said briskly. 'I'm needed in Doncaster. I'm driving up there this morning. You might sort out all the money side for me, though. Pension schemes and whatnot at the *Technocrat*. Also spread the word about, I don't want to be bothered; phone calls, cards of sympathy, I'll take it all as read. Now I'll just make myself a cup of coffee. Then I'll get packed and be off.'

She walked over to the sink, picked up the kettle, turned on the tap. As she watched the water bubbling and foaming into echoing metal, she felt giddy and light-headed as though on a great height overlooking a torrent. Strange images invaded her mind; stabbing Monk at the funeral with the razor-edged kitchen knife and so bringing the whole business out in the open; eloping with Trevor by ladder and horseback and running away to Brussels; becoming an intelligence agent and spending all her nights meeting scientists on Town Field; entering Danny-boy at Cruft's and beating her father in the world snooker final; rolling naked around the floor of a Doncaster coffee shop holding Sally Ann Hibbert in a lesbian embrace; and just when it seemed that these images must burst out of her bubbling brain as the water was foaming over the top of the kettle, she was violently sick in the washing-up basin, and after that she felt much better.

24

The two children regarded each other warily. The girl was older, just able to toddle, and age and mobility should have given her the edge over the little boy in the carry-cot. But something in the set of his jaw and the most unbaby-like steadiness with which he observed her tottering approach gave promise of a will not easily overawed.

Jennifer Challenger drank her coffee and smiled at the girl with proprietary pride.

'The doctor says he's never known a kiddie so advanced,' she said.

'Yes,' agreed Mrs Haddington. 'After the boys already.'

Jennifer was armoured with the confidence of successful motherhood and a restored figure, so she was only an iota malicious when she said, 'You'll miss Molly when she goes.'

'I can't complain. I've had her more than a year. She's seen me through,' said Mrs Haddington.

So I have, thought Molly wonderingly, as she listened to the exchange from the other side of the table. After all these years she had at last been able to give something back to this sturdily independent woman.

First there had been the news of Sam's death. Far from being a debilitating factor, the awareness of her daughter's loss and her need for comfort and support had seemed to accelerate Mrs Haddington's recovery. Her own illness became merely a kudos-accruing counter to any effort by her friends to command attention with their minor ailments, and if Molly's bereavement had not been psychological therapy enough, the news of her pregnancy had provided a superabundance.

'There, there, Samkin,' said Mrs Haddington, making a quite unnecessary adjustment to his woolly jacket. 'He's growing out of that already, Molly. He'll need a new one just now.'

'I'll give you some of Terry's, Molly,' said Jennifer. 'She's shooting up at such a rate too.'

'No, thank you,' said Mrs Haddington firmly. 'No cast-offs for our Samkin. No offence, Jennifer.'

Jennifer and Molly exchanged the rueful smile of those who know all there is to know about grandmothers. They could never be friends but there was no reason why from time to time they should not be allies. The news of Sam's death had brought a wild hope to Trevor; Molly knew this for he had told her; she could only guess at the wild fear it had brought to Jennifer.

The news of Molly's pregnancy had changed everything. Or perhaps not, for she liked to think that in the end she would not have had the egoism to break up the Challenger family even if she had the desire. That's what she liked to think but she had developed a sharp eye for disguises now, even her own.

Trevor's last fling had been to suggest it might be his. She had laughed and lied, saying that with lovers she always took double precautions. In fact Trevor was the two-to-one-on favourite. She and Sam had made love only once since her last period. His mind had been on other things.

Young Sam (or Samkin, as his grandmother had unilaterally christened him) certainly had Trevor's colouring, but then Terry, his own daughter, was black-haired and sallow-skinned, a throw back (Mrs Haddington hinted) to Jennifer's gypsy forebears. If they *were* half-brother and half-sister, thought Molly, there was scope here for one of those nice romantic plots in seventeen or eighteen years' time. But that was too far ahead to worry about, and she doubted if she would worry all that much anyway. At the moment she was content to keep just enough of the road ahead in sight as was necessary for safe driving.

The *coup de grâce* to both wild hope and wild fear in the Challenger family had been the news of Molly's engagement.

The first couple of months at home had run smoothly with Molly at the helm, Ivor back in his old familiar groove of work, telly and the Club, and Mrs Haddington almost having to be anchored down to prevent a too rapid re-assumption of the primacy. This was what bothered Molly most – not her mother's recovery, which was a source of great joy – but the prospect of bringing up a baby in a house run by a fully fit, over-long repressed grandmother. The obvious solution was to set up her own separate establishment once the baby had been born – but there were snags here too, mainly financial. Sam had left a little money, no property (the Westcliff house had been rented), no pension (he had opted out of, or rather never opted in to *The New Technocrat* superannuation scheme) and no insurance. There had been policies, two large ones, taken out at the time of his marriage. The premiums on both had fallen due a month before his disappearance. They had not been paid. It was as if Sam had ceased to believe in an insurable future as soon as he heard that Leskov had named him.

Well, he had been right, thought Molly. Now she was able to see that the money in the bank plus what came from the sale of much of the Westcliff house furniture, plus an ex-gratia payment of six months' salary from *The New Technocrat*, left her much more comfortably placed than thousands of other newly-widowed women. But then, at a point in her pregnancy when she seemed to feel sick all the time and the months ahead stretched interminably, she had felt herself to be a pauper, condemned to live on the charity of others for ever.

Her response had been, characteristically, not to fall into a fit of deep depression, but to find herself first irritated, then indignant, then enraged at this set of circumstances.

Rising to pee in the middle of the night was proving another trial of her condition. At three o'clock one morning, instead of returning to bed, she tiptoed downstairs, sat at the kitchen table, put a piece of paper in Sam's old portable typewriter and wrote a letter.

Dear Ambassador,
   It is my understanding that my late husband, Sam Keatley, Defence Correspondent of *The New Technocrat*, was in the employ of your government for the past twenty years. I assume that in a socialist state arrangements exist to compensate the dependents of those who die while on state service and I look forward to hearing what kind of settlement

your government feels appropriate in the present case.

Yours sincerely,

Molly Keatley

She then addressed an envelope to the Soviet Embassy, getting the address from her old London *vade-mecum*, stamped it, slipped on her sheepskin coat over her nightgown, and went out to the letter-box at the end of the street and posted it.

As she walked back in the chill, quiet darkness, she was already regretting the impulse. The post was lifted at eight o'clock in the morning and she resolved to be there a couple of minutes beforehand with some story prepared to coax the postman into letting her retrieve the letter.

But when she awoke it was after nine. Her alarm clock had stopped, Ivor had had to make his own breakfast, her mother was playing her radio at full blast as a gentle hint and Danny-boy was scrabbling at the bedroom door.

Sod it! she thought. They'll likely just rip it up anyway.

And she got briskly out of bed and set about preparing breakfast, not realizing until half an hour later that she hadn't been sick and indeed felt better than she had done for months.

A fortnight later the doorbell rang.

It was Monk.

She hadn't seen him since the funeral which had been surprisingly bearable. The grief she felt for Sam had so little to do with the circumstances imagined by the majority of those present that she was able to draw an almost gleeful strength from the difference, like a child with a powerful secret. The glee had been near-hysterical, of course, as when she had to stuff her handkerchief into her mouth as the vicar developed the theme of the responsible journalist being a pillar of democracy. Only the shame of being the cause of such embarrassed anxiety on Ivor's face made her pull herself together.

Afterwards she had been perfectly calm. Monk had shaken her hand in his turn and she had recalled that this was the moment when she had thought of slipping the knife into his belly. But she hadn't. She had learned the day before that she was pregnant. In any case Monk had put on what looked like a new black suit and white shirt and it would have been a shame to spoil it.

He wore the same suit now as he stood on the doorstep. It looked as if it had been carefully stored away since the funeral and only brought out that morning. Molly felt almost touched.

Ignoring her mother's wildly inquisitive face Molly had shut the living-room door firmly and led her visitor into the cold front parlour.

'How are you, missus?' said Monk.

'I'm fine. Yourself?'

'Bearing up,' he said. 'I heard you were expecting.'

'It's getting hard to conceal,' said Molly.

'Are you pleased?'

She smiled at his directness.

'I'll see how it goes,' she said. 'What do you want, Mr Monk? To be a godfather?'

For an answer he reached into his inside pocket, drew out a large buff envelope from which in turn he produced Molly's letter to the Russian Embassy.

'Who did you say you were working for?' she asked.

'They passed it on. I think you'd embarrassed them, missus. Funny, that.'

He grinned suddenly. It was a wolfish, toothy kind of grin but not unattractive. It went as quickly as it had come when she did not respond.

'And they've passed on the embarrassment to you,' said Molly. 'All right.'

She plucked the letter from his hands and tore it into eight pieces.

'There,' she said. 'Now you're disembarrassed.'

He took the torn fragments from her and carefully replaced them in the buff envelope.

'For the files?' she said.

'No, missus,' he said. 'A memento. Else, who would believe it?'

Now she smiled and after a moment the wolfish grin re-appeared.

'How hard up are you, missus?' he asked.

'I have a little capital and what the State doles out to me each week,' said Molly. 'I'll survive.'

'I never doubted that,' said Monk. 'I'll be off now.'

The living-room door was ajar as Molly showed him out.

'Do you know who he reminds me of?' said Mrs Haddington.

'Go on, Mum. Amaze me.'

'Sam. Oh yes. Don't look at me as if I'm daft. Same eyes and mouth. Reliable. You look if he comes again.'

'Oh Mum! You need your glasses. And he's not coming again.'

But he did. She looked uncomprehendingly at the bit of paper he gave her, understanding only the figure of five thousand pounds.

'It's a money draft, missus.'

'Hush money?'

'Just a draft. Not traceable.'

'Why should I want to trace it?'

'Because you're not going to take much on trust any more, missus. You'll have to take this on trust, though.'

'Do I have to sign anything?'

He shook his head.

'No strings,' he said. 'Do what you want with it. Save it till your kiddie's eighteen if you want.'

She looked at him scornfully.

'You must be joking! By that time I hope I'll have found someone else to foot the bills!'

She couldn't understand what had made her say that. Thoughts of remarriage had never even crossed her mind. Her mother had said one evening, 'Some day, happen, you never know . . .' and Molly had felt the proposition too absurd to be worth refuting.

'Here you are then.'

He gave her the draft. In the hall they had a 'chance' encounter with Mrs Haddington, looking frail and haggard still. Monk assured her how well she looked. Mrs Haddington thanked him kindly and then proceeded to make oblique enquiries as to his provenance and business. Molly watched with amusement this courteous encounter between the queen of interrogation and the king of evasion. But she ceased to be amused when she heard her mother inviting Monk to stay for lunch. He glanced towards her.

'It's just tinned Irish Stew,' she said. 'I've grown very fond of tinned Irish Stew.'

'My favourite, missus,' said Monk.

He ate as if he meant it.

'There. What did I tell you?' said Mrs Haddington afterwards. 'Sam's eyes.'

'Not that again!' said Molly.

'You please yourself,' said her mother. 'But he has. And I'll tell you another thing. He fancies you.'

The idea was so monstrous that Molly could not take it in.

When Monk rang two days later, ostensibly just to thank her for the lunch, she said right out, 'Mr Monk, my mother thinks you fancy me. Sexually, I mean.'

'I'm afraid so, missus,' answered Monk without hesitation. 'I wouldn't have said ought myself, not yet awhile, you understand. But seeing how you've asked me direct, I won't deny it.'

'You must be mad!' cried Molly.

'Mad? Why? I'm no oil painting, missus, but I've got my own teeth.'

'Not you. Me! I mean, look at me. Daily I grow more inaccessible!'

'I'm a patient man, missus. Hard work and cold showers can do wonders.'

It was a joke and Molly found herself smiling. Perhaps she should have said what she had really been thinking. He was mad like that hunchbacked king in the play had been mad when he wooed the wife of the man he'd just murdered over his coffin. Richard the Third. She had little enthusiasm for the stage but Sam had taken her. She had enjoyed it without being in the least convinced.

Now she was convinced without in the least enjoying it.

A lie, she admonished herself. She was amused, flattered even. It doubled her admirers, though not her hope. Monk and Trevor. Trevor was possible but now, somehow, out of the question. Monk was impossible, but he was very much in the question. He had suggested she should spend a day shopping in London and have lunch with him and instead of refusing outright she replied, 'What have I got to shop for? Or with?'

'You got a draft for five thousand pounds.'

'I haven't done anything about that yet.'

'I know, missus. Up to you. Either way, you'll still want to stock up with baby things.'

She reacted with Yorkshire scorn.

'What's London got I can't buy in Doncaster at half the price?'

'They say Oxford Street's like the casbah these days,' he answered. 'You can probably get swaddling clothes there.'

That made her laugh and when he took the laughter as agreement and went on to fix a day, she didn't disagree.

Over lunch he told her about himself. To her surprise he revealed that he was a widower. His wife had died twelve years earlier of a brain tumour.

'Did she know what you were? Your job, I mean?'

'A lot less than you, missus,' said Monk.

'Would you have told her?'

He looked at her assessingly, very clerk-of-works.

'You're thinking of Sam,' he said. 'It's a lot different.'

'Is it? Never to know, that's the same.'

'It's a comfortable way to live.'

'It's a mockery,' she said fiercely.

'Mebbe. Well, you know now. About Sam and about me.'

This association angered her.

'I know Sam's dead and you're alive, Mr Monk,' she said.

'You still blame me?'

She would have liked to say 'yes' but honesty is a difficult path to leave.

'There's a chain,' she said. 'You're somewhere in it, but there're lots of links. I'm in it too.'

'You?'

'Oh yes,' she said bitterly. 'I had a chance to tell him yes, I'd come and live with him in Russia or no, go to hell. But I didn't. I left it hanging and he came again and . . .'

She saw it again, the blue car, the bloody road. She had kept it from her mind for weeks now.

'Which were you going to say?' asked Monk.

'What? I don't know. How should I know? I wanted to say yes, but at the same time I wanted it finished. A clean break, one amputation, finish. That sounds brave, doesn't it? But at the back of my mind, now I look back at it, I wonder if it wasn't just fear. The thought of moving, of starting again in a foreign country, in Moscow. I wonder if I got my husband killed just because I didn't want to move to Moscow! It's like getting someone killed because you don't want to move to Margate!'

'Hardly that,' he said. 'Do you want some pudding?'

Their relationship had firmed up rather than advanced, she told herself on the homeward train. Which was the most he could hope for. They might become better acquainted, but there was nowhere for them to go.

For all that she felt piqued when there was no word from him for a fortnight. Then he turned up on the doorstep again. It was early one evening. He made himself comfortable in front of the television, chatted amiably to Mrs Haddington, ate the dropscones and drank the cocoa offered to him, took a glass of whisky with Ivor when he returned from the Club and rose to go at half past eleven.

At the front door he said to Molly, 'I'm stopping at the York Hotel. Come and have coffee or a drink there in the morning.'

Molly had been wondering whether he proposed driving back to London that night but had not mentioned it for fear that her mother would invite him to stay. Now she felt guilty so she agreed to meet him.

Back in the living-room her mother said, 'He's a nice chap, that Morris.'

'Who?'

'*Morris*,' said her mother. 'You really should be calling him by his given name now, Molly. What do you think, Father?'

'He seems very steady,' said Ivor. 'Knows summat about pigeons.'

'Oh God,' said Molly. 'You're a pair of panders.'

But next day when they met she called him Morris, if only she explained, to prevent him from ever calling her 'missus' again.

And that was that, as far as she was concerned. The last step forward. They were friends, they met fairly often, they were comfortable with each other, they never touched sexually, but they laughed together frequently, she at him and he at the follies of the world. He did not grow more handsome or younger

190

in her sight, but her awareness of the difference between what he was and what he looked brought back to her something of the inward glee she had experienced at Sam's funeral though this time without any of the attendant hysteria.

The night after the baby was born, she woke in the twilit hospital ward and knew that all the glee and all the laughter and all the comfort she had felt in the past few months was a betrayal of Sam and would have to be paid for. She started to weep and could not stop. Tranquillized, she slept, but woke again to tears. The consultant explained it all to her in simple language. She didn't bother to explain it to the consultant. She knew herself now better than any of the magi the National Health Service could bring to her bedside, and knew that her tears would surely end.

They stopped the following day when Monk appeared with a bunch of tired violets in his hand and a half-bottle of whisky in his jacket pocket.

He examined the baby with interest.

'Healthy,' he said.

'You like the look of him?' asked Molly.

'A lot,' he said.

'Right. You've got first refusal,' she said.

'What's the price?'

'Five thousand pounds?' she suggested.

'Done,' he said.

'Morris and I are getting married,' said Molly when her mother arrived a few minutes later.

'Yes, he told me,' said Mrs Haddington. 'How's my little Samkin then? Hello, my lovely. He knows his old granny already. Look at him smile.'

'Look at him smile. He knows his old granny,' said Mrs Haddington. 'See if you can get our bill, Molly. It's that lass with the funny eye. She lives in a world of her own, that one. I think she's a Telford out of Goole. They're all a bit cracked in that family.'

'I'll see to it,' offered Jennifer. 'I'm meeting Trevor here so there's no hurry.'

'That's kind of you, Jennifer,' said Mrs Haddington. 'We've

got to be back for Ivor. Come on, Samkin. Say bye-bye to Terry.'

She started fussing over the carry-cot.

' 'Bye Molly,' said Jennifer. 'I'll let you have those things.' She nodded significantly at Samkin.

'In a plain brown paper wrapping,' said Molly, smiling. ''Bye.'

They met Trevor on the way out. He was standing at the *parfumerie* counter talking to a salesgirl made up like a marionette. He waved at them as they passed but made no effort to break off his suave man-of-the-world intercourse.

I've helped make him like this, thought Molly with a little frown. Twice I've abandoned him.

Then she smiled at her arrogance.

Monk arrived late that afternoon. He was particularly busy at the moment in anticipation of leaving his current job.

'Nought to do with you,' he assured her. 'It's just the time of life. I'm getting too old to work in the field. Late hours, secret meetings, all that. It's no use if you're falling to sleep all the time.'

'So they're kicking you upstairs?'

'In a way. Putting me behind a desk, anyway. Only thing is . . .'

'Yes?'

'The desk might be abroad. Do you mind?'

Molly thought about it. She didn't really mind. She had no great desire to live in London again. On the other hand she didn't want to be too far from her mother, whose health, though apparently almost completely recovered, was still a cause of concern. But she accepted Monk's assurance that home leave was good and in any case nowhere was more than a few hours' flying time away.

That night after her parents had diplomatically retired to bed (most of the diplomacy emanating from her mother) she and Monk sat together in the living-room on the little comfortable sofa in front of the fire.

'Penny for them,' said Monk.

'I was wondering why I was marrying you,' said Molly.

Monk laughed, disturbing Danny-boy, asleep under the table.

'I know why I'm marrying you, missus,' he said broadly. 'It's answers like that.'

'Aggressive?' she said.

'Honest,' he said.

'Same thing,' she said. 'But it's necessary. Be warned. I'll do for the next man who deceives me.'

She tried to speak lightly but the thought went through her mind, *like I did for the last one*, and she wondered if Monk was thinking it too.

'Why are you marrying me then?' he asked.

'God knows. No, that sounds rude. But everything's going to sound rude. I like older men? Help! I'm thirty-four and have got a baby and there won't be many offers. Worse! I don't know. You feel . . . reliable. I need a bit of strength outside myself. Is that any better?'

'It's all right for starters.'

He put his arm around her shoulders.

This and the exchange of rather aseptic kisses on meeting and parting was as far as their physical contact had gone. Since Samkin's birth Molly had not felt ready either physically or mentally for the rigours of sex. But now, quite suddenly, she felt a need for . . . something, she was not quite sure what, but she turned her face up to Monk's pale commonplace features and invited his lips to press down on hers, and her response was so fierce that after a few bruising moments, he tried to draw her down on to the white mohair rug in front of the fire.

'No,' she whispered. 'It's not decent. Upstairs.'

Taking his hand, she led him up the stairs. Half way up a loose board let out a loud creak and she got a fit of the giggles. Behind her, rather to her surprise and also to her pleasure, she heard Monk giggling too.

Samkin was gurgling in his cot in the corner of her bedroom. She hesitated in the doorway. Would their lovemaking wake him and perhaps leave an indelible noise-print on his subconscious? Or would he start crying at a crucial stage and ruin this first night?

Monk bumped into her impatiently.

'Come on, missus!' he urged.

She went on and undressed rapidly in the dark. Lying naked between the cold sheets of the old high bed, she became aware that Monk was draping his clothes meticulously over a bedside chair.

'Come on, mister!' she commanded.

He came on. At first the touch and exploration of this new body was fascinating. But when he lay on top of her, and in her, and bound her to him, and she him to her, with strong arms and legs, the thought popped into her mind that it might as well be Sam. Or Trevor. Or . . . surely there were no other 'ors'? Did it matter that she felt like this? It wasn't that she was blinded by lust. There was going to be no orgasm this time, she quickly realized, but her need had not after all been for a simple sexual release. What she had suddenly wanted so desperately was what she had got, the closest possible physical contact without words, without ideas, without reason. Reason draws us into the past, hales us into the future, she thought. The senses bind us to the here and now. And yet the mind will not be still. These lips on mine, these hands on my buttocks, that length of blood-gorged muscle between my thighs, these things I feel and enjoy and respond to without pretence. Yet my mind runs on, like a passenger in a dimly lit railway carriage going through a very long and dark tunnel, so dark and so long that after a while the passenger no longer knows if she has her back or her face to the engine.

Do I love him? she considered. Do I have data enough to decide? I thought I knew Trevor, yet he changed. I thought I knew Sam, yet he prevaricated. Mutation, equivocation, what's it matter so long as he's a nice boy and loves my mother? Mother, mother, Holy Mother, Russia. Oh Sam, suppose I'd said yes, straightaway, without thought, yes, I'll come with you now and live with you in an igloo in Holy Mother Russia. You, me, Samkin. Would you have believed in Samkin? Would it have mattered . . . perhaps . . . Samkin in the snow . . . Samkin on a sledge . . . Samkin a Russian . . . and Sam . . . no, perhaps all was for the best . . . what best . . . this best . . . no best . . . Sam in the street . . . Sam smiling . . . the blue car . . . round the corner . . . the blue car . . . round the corner . . . car corner car corner car . . .

She felt Monk expand inside her and even as she cried out at the pain of her thought rather than the pleasure of her senses, the rational creature in the railway carriage was able to remark coolly how well timed it had all been.

Then the train was out of the tunnel and she was straining her ears to see if they had woken Samkin.

No, he gurgled on. Monk moved off her body and lay by her side barely touching her.

'How was it?' she said.

'Good,' he said. 'And you?'

'Mind your own business,' she answered mockingly, but at the same time she realized, not happily, she meant it. One's own business must be minded.

In silence they lay for a while.

In her mind she heard herself asking Monk for the last time ever 'Did you have Sam killed?'

'No,' she heard him reply without a pause for thought.

'Then it must have been me,' she said aloud.

'What?'

'Nothing. I talk in my sleep. You'll have to get used to it.'

'My pleasure,' he said.

A little later he said so casually that she was instantly alerted, 'Oh, by the way, I got a bit of news today.'

'Yes?'

'About my new job. I'm to be a third trade secretary, some such thing.'

'What on earth's that?'

'It means being in charge of local agents at one of our embassies.'

'You said you wouldn't be doing undercover work in the field!' she protested.

'I'll hardly leave my office,' he answered. 'And there's nought undercover about it. Everybody knows. The title's just a convention.'

'Oh well, that's all right then. Where's it to be. Timbuctoo?'

'No,' he said. 'Moscow.'

She went very still, stiff almost.

'Look, I'm sorry about it. I could turn it down, but I don't want to. It's real work. Timbuctoo's not real work. The world's full of Timbuctoos. But you say what you think. Living in

Russia, is that out of the question for you?'

She didn't speak but she turned to him and curled into a foetal ball so that her knees and the top of her head together pressed against his flat taut belly. Something was happening inside her but when it came out she scarcely knew whether she was laughing or crying, any more than Monk, who switched on the bedside light and regarded with nonplussed concern the convulsive rise and fall of her naked shoulders.

About the Author

Reginald Hill was born in 1936 in West Hartlepool, England, and raised in Carlisle. Educated at Oxford, he now teaches in the English Department of the Doncaster College of Education. *The Spy's Wife* is Hill's eighth mystery. His previous books include *A Pinch of Snuff* and *Ruling Passion*.